I0531627

Storylandia

The Wapshott Journal
of Fiction

Issue 36

The Wapshott Press

Storylandia, Issue 36, The Wapshott Journal of Fiction, ISSN 1947-5349, ISBN 978-1-942007-35-7 is published at intervals by the Wapshott Press, now a 501(c)(3) nonprofit, PO Box 31513, Los Angeles, California, 90031-0513, telephone 323-201-7147. All correspondence can be sent to The Wapshott Press, PO Box 31513, LA CA 90031-0513. Visit our website at www.WapshottPress.org to learn more. This work is copyright © 2021 by Storylandia. The Wapshott Journal of Fiction, Los Angeles, California. Copyright © 2000-2020 by individual authors and is reprinted here with the copyright owners' permission.

Storylandia is always seeking quality original short stories, novelettes, and novellas. Please have a look at our submission guidelines at www.Storylandia.WapshottPress.org or email the editor at editor@wapshottpress.org

Donations happily accepted at www.donate.wapshottpress.org

Cover image: "Nostalgia," by Samuel Ferri. www.misconnected.com

The DeDramafi was originally published on The Write Launch in 2019 and is republished here with permission.

Storylandia

The Wapshott Journal of Fiction

Founded in 2009

Issue 36, Winter 2021

Edited by Ginger Mayerson

Contents

Storylandia
Issue 36

by
Bob Ritchie
Gordon J. Stirling
John O'Kane
Evan Howell
Jhon Sánchez

Bob Ritchie

The Ear Is the Way to the Soul

I first thought there could be a God when I was in a church. Fitting perhaps, but entirely coincidental. I had believed myself an atheist (this, in Redlands, California—a town not known for its liberalism) since the tender age of nine, when I realized that all the organized religions to which I'd thus far been exposed—the Presbyterian, Catholic, Episcopalian, Methodist, and Baptist faiths—were a crock. To put it neatly. Each seemed to be a way to pay hypocritical lip-service to an unlikely grandfatherly figure. One should not embrace such skepticism at age nine, but I already had the scoop on Santa Claus, the Tooth Fairy, and the Easter Bunny. God fell quickly after those three venerable—and more generous—beings went the way of my innocence.

Eight years later, the fact that I vehemently did not believe in God became a constant bone of contention between Lisa and me.

"How can you not?" she would ask. Usually as we cuddled together on the green and flower-covered sofa in her family's parlor. Usually when I started to get especially hot under the belt buckle and she felt the need to slow the pace a little.

As a relatively normal high school male, I was anxious to unload the heavy burden of my virginity. Lisa did not feel the need as urgently, believing—as her parents and her God had taught her—that one must wait for marriage.

"Come on, Lisa," I would wheedle. The eyes that looked into mine were wide and deep—even when disagreeing—I felt I could swim in their ocean-green depths, "God is a myth perpetuated by the weak-minded and greedy. Show me proof one of His/Her/Its existence, and I'll reconsider." Her abrupt cessation of kissing and touching always cooled my ardor but warmed my temper.

"Of course, He does," she would state with finality, proffering none of the requested proof, but instead wrinkling her small nose and squinting her eyes, as if those acts alone would win the day. And she was so damned beautiful, they almost did. Unaware that I was doing so, I began to reconsider my beliefs. Question them.

This scene occurred more than once. With interesting variations. And throughout our relationship, we replayed it more and more often, until we reached a point where our very real love for each other supplanted the issue.

With my relationship more or less at a standstill, my realization that there might be a God arrived at a time when I was vulnerable to new possibilities.

The First Methodist Church on Church Corners in Redlands is a huge brick box of a place. A behemoth. It was constructed with a view toward more than just simple worship. Rails and struts crisscross the 40-foot-high ceiling, perfect for hanging lights, equipment, and backdrops. There is even a car that depends from the rails and scoots you across these amazing heights so that the lights can be mounted, focused, turned; so banners and backdrops can be hung from the support rods. Sanctuary may be its official *nom de plume*, but *theater* would be an appropriate appellation.

Boasting amazing acoustics, the sanctuary had housed the choirs to which I once belonged (due mostly to the fact that the Redlands Senior High School Chorus teacher—Mr. Vijo—also wore the hat of music director for the church). The sweet teenage voices of the Redlands High School Show Singers, Classical Singers, and Girls' Choir were well known and received there.

Mr. Vijo, as the music director, had insisted on the purchase of a full 9-foot Steinway concert grand piano. And what an organ the place had! The pipes ranged from the tall and silvery and majestic to the tiny, whistle-like deelies that tweeted in the same way as a blown-on blade of grass between the thumbs. Though not a keyboard technician, I pounded and played the organ with noisy abandon. In the dark and with the church as empty as my soul was purported to be. My solitude I filled with the stunning tones that rang through the darkness. I played like a musical ghost, haunting the corners with transparent eighth notes and spooking children passing on the sidewalk outside with thunderous chord-clusters. Not only that, but my improvisations were atrocious, so if someone happened in, they were in for a fright. Still, playing the organ—filling myself with grand tones and heavy bass—was a wonderfully cathartic experience. One that I needed. I suppose that made me no more or less neurotic than my compatriots.... But that's a relative statement; teenagers are escaped loonies, all. The organ functioned as psychiatrist and priest, at a time when I believed in neither.

And on it, I could play out my passions. Never having used my own, the majestic instrument acted as an explosive and fitting—if not completely satisfying—alternative to the big "S."

Transported on the wings of my playing one fine Friday night, I stopped at Sandford's shouted command. "Relsin, give it a rest!"

Reluctantly, I brought my fingers to a hover several inches above the bottom rank, "What's up?" I shouted back. His voice came from below and under the balcony in what passed for the tech room. It was a crowded space filled with out-of-date electronics, candleholders, sheet music, and the odd choir robe or two. I watched a drop of sweat fall from my face and splash on the back of my splay-fingered hand. Summer nights in Redlands are nearly as hot as summer days.

As I waited, I reflected on Sandford Granpen, friend.

Sandford is ten years older than I am and somehow manages to look younger. Completely asexual, he is a whiz with computers, electronics, and music. He was one of those brilliant types who chooses obscurity and near poverty over fame and wealth. He could easily have had either or both, but for his shyness and the fact that he truly did not care. Perhaps the fact that he did not see himself as brilliant as others did also played a part in his life decision.

He lived a middle-of-the-road kind of life—calling Bingo on Saturdays at the local Y, singing in the church choir, reading nights, then going to bed. Looks also had come to him in mediocrity, medium-length brown hair—cut, but never styled. He stood 5'9", had green or hazel eyes (I could never be sure), and had these ears that just stuck their hands right out and said hello. Navy, grey, or dark brown polyester slacks paired with a variety of unexciting button-down shirts (short-sleeved in summer, long-sleeved in winter, both with breast-pocket) made up his outfit of choice. If his dress, habits, looks, and temperament reflected a certain simplicity, his choice of friends showed that he had a touch of the *outré:* witness his companions, Ben, Rich, and me.

We always pushed him to get out and do new stuff. Because of us, he eventually joined the local amateur circus. But that's another story.

So Sandford was fooling with the sound system in the cavernous and dark Great Hall. I had come along so I could play the organ and because Lisa was at her grandparents' house in San Diego. Well, we were arguing over sex again. Ben was here because we went everywhere together. San had brought along a tape in order to test the new (used) cassette deck the church had just purchased. The tape was *Something Horrible,* by Ferrante and Teicher. Blech!

Above and to my right, Ben sat in the ceiling cart. Not doing anything except staring at its clay-colored walls. He always operated under the thrall of one extreme mood or another. Like a manic/depressive, I suppose. His favorite extreme manifested itself as frequent outbursts of sullen and irrational anger. Today (or yesterday, who knows?) something either Sandford or I had done had apparently lit the short fuse of his temper.

When I decided I couldn't stand Ferrante and Teicher another second, which probably took all of a minute, I hopped down the balcony stairs, trotted through the back door and out to Ben's truck, and grabbed one of my tapes at random. Running back in, I saw that it was "Seconds Out," a live album by the group Genesis. Silently, I applauded my choice. I knew that Sandford didn't much care for "our" music, but my selfishness made me conveniently forget that fact. In the tech room, I said, "Here, play this, I can't handle that insipid yuch you're playing." With his usual accepting shrug, Sandford slotted the tape into the player.

It was cued up to a number called "Afterglow," a slow, dreamy piece I had always enjoyed but never found overly compelling.

When Sandford pressed "play," I walked into the Great Hall and waited for the tail end of the previous song to segue into "Afterglow." Have I mentioned that the room has great acoustics? Okay, yes, I'm sure I did.

The song starts simply enough, but in that place, in the dark and turned up loud enough to make my belly vibrate, the introduction became a stunning aural glimpse of what was to come. Yes, it sounded simple: guitar, keyboards, bass, drums, and voice. But the richness of their harmonies, of their rhythms playing one against the other, would have knocked me back in my seat had I been sitting. As it was, I staggered, put a hand on the back of a pew to keep myself from falling.

These were the days before "sampling" on synthesizers, but Tony Banks, the keyboard player, had a patch on one of his instruments that was intended to sound like a heavenly choir.

It did.

Unsurpassed beauty. Uncomplicated, rich... with a drifting though solid tempo (paradox, yeah, so sue me) that urged one up and up. As if, listening to it, you could climb the stairs to the very vault of heaven.

In the center of the hall, I stood. The smile on my face could not be measured. Tears stood in the corners of my eyes, just waiting for the go-ahead; my body felt full-to-bursting with... something. I didn't know then and still don't know now. God? Perhaps. All I can say is my heart sang, my stomach buzzed with hollow excitement, and my throat closed in on itself. I felt as if I could love the world. Quite a song.

Then it ended and life went on.

A few days later, Lisa and I did our regular dance of frustration. At my house this time. Alone.

I remember the stacks of books that lined my room. I read avidly in those days, not having the pressure of supporting myself gnawing at my attention. I remember the green bedspread with the raised fabric lines in it, like widely spaced corduroy. My window looked out on a spreading growth of ivy that—with the brightness of the midday sun—caused irregular shadows to dance and sway on the gold-shag carpet and white walls.

"C'mon Lisa. It's okay. Really. I mean, we love each other, right? And we want to get married. This is no more than a manifestation of our love." As much as I spoke the truth, I also uttered utter bullshit. You can use the truth as easily as a lie, if you work it right. And because the intent is coercion, it makes that truth ugly and false.

She lay against one of the bolster pillows on my bed. Her top and bra hung neatly from the back of my desk chair.

She had her arms crossed over her small, firm breasts. As if to warm or hide. It was not cold in the room, though the air conditioning was on "Arctic." I had seen her thus before. Right about now, the fun always came to a screeching halt. As if, while careening uncontrollably down a hill on a sled, the quick glimpse of cliff just ahead caused Lisa to turn us away from danger and send us tumbling—but safe—

through the cleansing and passion-cooling snow.

"No, Relly, it's against God. And my parents would kill me." She had that hard light in her eyes. I knew I had reached the point where I risked her eternal anger if I pushed any harder. The pain and strain in my groin blotted out the sensible voice in my mind. I heard myself starting that annoying whining, "Damn it, you always..."

Her eyes flashed fire, daring me to go on. I let out a whoosh of breath, shrugged tight shoulders and said, "Good grief, I... Aw, forget it!"

I turned and walked out of the room. *Perhaps a glass of orange juice will calm me*, I thought, *or an apple, or a dozen apples. Or six cold showers followed by a swift kick in the nuts.* I pitied myself my everlasting virginity, forgetting—as usual—how selfish I was being. By the time I reached the kitchen, my penis had relaxed, but I remained as tight as a clenched fist.

I opened the refrigerator ("reefer" my mom called it. I used to wonder whether she knew what that slang word meant) and moved the carton of low-fat milk out of the way. Behind, the bright orange of my favorite refreshment called cooling words. *Drink and relax,* it said. I took the plastic handle and brought the spout directly to my waiting mouth. Unwilling to release the anger, I shook my head before drinking and muttered, "'F I was any hornier, I'd screw a chocolate donut." Deep drink of sweet, cold. The open refrigerator sent out blasts of chill air as I quaffed and muttered by turns.

While grumbling to myself, I started in surprise when I felt two slender arms wrap themselves around my chest. I froze in place. The plastic jug of orange juice hung from my hand in mid air. Her cheek against my bare back felt warm and soft. She said something, too low for me to make out.

"What?"

"I said, I'm sorry."

I put the jug back on the shelf, turned into her embrace, loving the soft push of her breasts against my bare chest. "That's alright, I..." I hesitated, wondering at the growing feeling in my chest and stomach and throat. Much like... *exactly* like that which I had experienced in the Methodist Church only a few days before. Dizziness, a warmth, a fullness, a catch in the back of my throat, and the gathering of tears in my eyes. Not sadness. No. Voice gruff from emotion, I finished, "No, Lisa, *I'm* the one who should be sorry. You know, I... I love you so much. It's not that I want to hurt you, I just..." She was looking straight into my soul. Her wide-open eyes and completely relaxed face radiated a type of vulnerability that she had never shown. I felt the need for Truth, but not the type of truth I had always used to manipulate. "Well," I began, uncomfortable, but letting my voice carry me to an unfamiliar place, "I'm a teenage guy, and I'm hornier'n a dog in heat. It's how we are. I'm sorry. I'll leave you alone. I love you too much to hurt you any more." *Truth.* I made a silent promise to stand by my resolve no matter what. I had gone cold turkey on sugar the year before, and knew that however weak my will appeared at times, when I really worked at it, I could do 'most anything.

This feeling, this fullness, this belief that there might be a God loomed large. That and the mental repetition of my promise. Both so much so that I almost missed it.

Lisa laughed quietly. Through the laugh, tumbled soft words. The sound of her voice matched the fullness in my heart, "I know that's how you are. Do you think I don't feel the same? Do you think I don't want you as much as you want me?"

I had never thought of Lisa's feelings. I had never considered her own frustrations. "I never... It's as if all this time we were, like, on opposite teams, or something." I paused to let the thought reach fullness. Continued, "Instead of partners dealing with the same rules of the game." I smoothed her hair with one hand and ran the other up her bare back. She shivered at my touch.

"Let's... um, let's go back to your room." Her hand slid down and cupped my jean-covered buttock. She turned a little sideways and finger-walked the other down my chest, tickling my stomach with her long nails, resting her thumb on my belt buckle. On any other day, my self-involvement would have said, *Wow! I'm gonna get lucky! At last!* Instead, I raised my hand to her face, brushed the hair out of her eyes and said, "It has to be what *you* want. I love you no matter what. With or without." When I listen to my words right now, in the privacy of my keyboard, they remind me of the worst dialogue in the schmaltziest movie ever.

"I believe you," she said.

I did, too. I'm pretty sure that the awe and wonder in her voice, reflected by my surprised eyes, startled her.

"I believe you," she repeated. Her hand left my belt buckle and brushed against my chest like a feather. I shivered. She covered my hand with hers, stood on her toes and kissed me on the tip of my nose. A mischievous smile touched her lips and she tweaked my butt. "C'mon."

I'll never know what prompted her decision. In stories, these things are supposed to make sense. In order for there to be a Point B, there must have been a prior Point A. But real life never works out so neatly. Maybe it was enough for her to realize that I loved her. Maybe for the first time she realized she loved me. Maybe she decided that, just as most states have old laws in their books that no longer make sense in today's world, perhaps her God had some laws like that as well. Maybe, maybe, maybe...

"Relsin, where's the..." He broke off, waved a hand before my face, "Relsin, are you in there?"

The day after... the experience, Sandford and I went about preparing the folders of sheet music for our bell choir. Sandford pretended to be the director, and Ben, Rich, and I pretended to pay attention to his directions. We all managed to have a fabulous time. Something fun to do on Thursday nights. At the moment, Ben and Rich were off practicing Monty Python lines for the church talent show coming up on the weekend.

"Yeah, I... Listen, do you believe in God, San?"

He stopped, put down the ragged, black folder, and leaned against the director's podium. He shot me a quizzical look. Sanford had worn glasses when we met. And though a contact-lens man now, his eyes couldn't have been more owlish if he'd had on his old pair of glasses.

"I mean, you're one of those supremely intelligent human beings who seem to have it all together, know all you need to know. So I was thinking that if you believed in God, maybe you could tell me the reasons... the *proof* you've had, or whatever."

The middle C bell stood next to his resting hand on the purple velvet table. With his fingernail, he tinked the brass in a slow rhythm. I had never seen Sanford angry, embarrassed, or at a loss. "That's a very personal thing," he said, not angry, embarrassed, or at a loss. I wonder whether I saw his apparent unflappability as a challenge; Ben, Rich, and I would test it pretty strenuously in the near future. The air conditioner clicked off, and the room, cool and small, filled with silence.

"Oh, hey, I'm sorry, I didn't mean to offend you or..."

He interrupted, "No, what I mean to say is that the proof you want is a very personal thing. It comes from inside you. My reasons for my belief very probably wouldn't make a lick of sense to you, because they're *my* reasons."

"Oh."

We stood there, the heavy heat from the night melting through the closed windows, holding us in its velvet grip. Beyond our silence, the sounds of laughing kids and teens floated up from the movie theater exits that were diagonal to the bell-choir practice room. I recalled the richness of my two recent experiences and understood the truth of Sandford's statement: How likely was it that someone would understand that a song had brought me to a point nearing transcendence? The love—the true love—I had felt for the first time the night before would be easier to comprehend as a catalyst. But a song?

"Yeah, you're right."

We turned back to our efforts at organizing the mess of music.

Lisa and I never married. The passion of young love could not compete with age's clarity of thought.

Some years later, we met at the bank where she worked. She told me that she had never regretted her decision.

Nice to hear. I wonder whether you can understand why I never regretted it either. Well, for a teenage boy, losing one's virginity is an important milestone. But no, that ain't it. Some people—and I hate to admit it, but I am one—need proof of even the most obvious "realities": The vulnerability that love brings won't kill you.

I looked at the four silver-framed headshots that protected the wide expanse of her desk from the rest of the world: three kids and a husband. I smiled my sincere smile, said my sincere words, walked away.

I shall forever remember those two experiences. When I play the same song on my computer, I feel an echo of that same transcendent beauty, a kind of low-key reminder.

I can no longer claim atheism as my religion, though only four times more have I known God. Each time, either love or music acted as herald to that (alleged) Supreme Being. I had a six-year wait after graduating high school, but the day that I met and fell eye-deep in love with a wonderful and beautiful Puerto Rican girl named Arlín qualifies as "awareness of God" in my heart; once, at a "Yes" concert in Worcester, Mass., during the song "Awaken," the power of the music lifted me up and over the barriers to God that I've erected—and that stand, still, if at a lower height—in my soul; once, when my father stepped through the American Airlines exit gate in San Juan, Puerto Rico, the swelling in my chest could not be blamed on spicy food. Most recently, I felt God's existence in the studio as I recorded my first demo tape.

I expect I will have God in my heart/soul again. I know that someday I will be able to sustain the feeling instead of having this day-to-day questioning that is my current reality. Does that make me an agnostic? What a contradiction.

I think back on the events and see that the common denominators are surpassing beauty and surpassing love. If there is a God, I can't imagine that It/He/She is a terrible, wrathful being. If there is a God, then It/He/She is in the songs that touch me most deeply, such as "Afterglow" and "Awaken"; is in my love for my father, mother, sister, children; is in the eyes, touch, being of Lisa and Arlín.

Gordon Stirling

The School's on Fire!

The TV announcers were droning during a dull Sunday afternoon ballgame. After lunch in the recliner my eyes were closing. I was surrendering to a well-deserved nap. I'd settled a tough insurance case Friday that dragged on too long. My law practice in the small town where I grew up, across the bay from San Francisco, was going well, but some cases wore me out.

I'm not sure how long I'd dozed when I was roused awake by kids' voices yelling up and down the block outside and a jumble of pounding footsteps. I shook my head to clear it and scrambled from the chair to open the front door. I yelled, "What's going on?" to a boy racing down the street. Still running, he didn't even look at me. "The school's on fire! The school's on fire!" he shouted.

I looked in the direction of the grade school a few blocks away. There was a brownish-gray plume of smoke over that way, a bruise against the blue June sky. I smelled the smoke on the bay breeze. From my doorway I watched groups of kids running toward the school, red-faced as they sprinted, giddy and laughing at the idea of the school burning down.

I'm human. We like to watch fires. I put on shoes and a jacket and went to see this one. On a Sunday, no students or staff were in danger but I hoped damage would be light.

The school is a little gem. Spacious, with open-air hallways and terraced buildings facing the bay, it was perfectly designed for its coastal hills setting. I broke into a trot to get to the school faster. People were converging on the fire from three directions, walking, or crowding their cars half up on sidewalks on both sides of our narrow, hilly streets.

The traffic circle outside the school's main office building swarmed with parents, kids and police cars. Fire trucks crushed against the traffic circle curb. Fire fighters ran to find good hose angles to spray toward the school office. It was ablaze.

Kids were running and weaving around the grown-ups and the fire trucks, inside and outside the rope line the cops set up, shouting with uncontainable energy. Their one glorious hope was that school days would be canceled. Neither parents nor cops were succeeding, or even trying very hard, to control them.

But amidst the glee of the kids there was disquiet, and whispers. An undercurrent of rumor with a name attached. "Robbie Elkins," a boy told another. Robbie's name kept snaking through the crowd. Someone thought they'd seen him near the school before the fire.

I knew Robbie a little. Quiet, not an athlete, kind of a peripheral kid. His dad was said to be pretty strict with Robbie and his sister Mags. The past couple of months, his last at the grade school, I'd thought Robbie might be rebelling a little against his parents. His hair had gotten longer. I'd seen him wearing some rock band t-shirts. I couldn't imagine him, though, an

11-year-old arsonist.

It was bad to have a kid's name attached to a serious crime. It would be hung around his neck for a long time. If he'd done it; but I didn't know if he'd done it. I didn't see any of the Elkins family at the school.

The fire got put out, limited to the school office. Both fire and water damage looked extensive. I guessed school admin would be run out of a trailer for a while. Old Man Clark, the principal, had a hard time keeping back of the rope line. He wanted to see what was lost. File cabinets, payroll, maintenance records, it all agitated him.

The school kids, and the young parents who'd also had him as principal, enjoyed the sight. Payback for anxiety induced in two generations. He was not an easy guy. He'd put on weight the past couple of years, drinking some. I'd heard the assistant principal had to sober him up with coffee before PTA meetings.

It got dark and near dinner time, and the fire department was done, so the crowd dispersed. Police officers spoke to some of those who'd said Robbie's name. If the fire wasn't an accident, I hoped the cops could speak to Robbie that night and put the rumors about his involvement to rest.

I was up early on Monday; I had to be at the courthouse downtown to ask for a continuance on a case. The corridor talk in the building troubled me. The cops had found the source of the fire—a gasoline trail leading from a window on the backside of the school office to the files with student records. The fire was deliberate.

Worse, Robbie Elkins hadn't come home. His folks hadn't seen him since Sunday afternoon, when he said he was going to the playground to see if anyone was playing ball. Robbie Elkins was wanted on suspicion for the fire. He was on the run.

I didn't want to think of Robbie scared, desperate, in hiding. If he'd set the fire and thought he'd be caught, he'd be thinking the worst—really angry parents and juvie - fears that make kids run away. I didn't know the family well, but I wanted to help if I could. There had to be a back story that led to this.

I was at a fast food place around the corner from my office getting lunch when I saw Mags come in with a group of girls. It looked like she was sort of floating in the middle of them, like they were buoying her in a time of trouble.

I called out to her. Mags broke off from her group and came over. I asked how she and her family were doing. "We're scared," she said. "We don't know where my brother is." It'd been 24 hours since the fire. "My mom is crying, I've never seen her cry," Mags continued, tears welling up. "Do you know what happened?" I asked. "I know what people are saying about him and the fire," she replied, "but we don't know anything about that. He was upset about something that happened at school but he wouldn't say what."

"Please tell your mom and dad you saw me and I said I'd help if I could," I asked. "To find him, or to help him with the police, or anything." A tearful smile from Mags. "Ok," she answered, "I will. They'll like that." She went to sit with her friends.

I pondered what Mags said. Maybe there was a connection between whatever problem Robbie had at school, and the fire and Robbie running away. All that could be sorted out, but first, we had to find him. A kid that age on the road wasn't safe.

By mid-week, three days after the fire, and with still no word on Robbie's whereabouts, I became increasingly worried. I hoped he hadn't hurt himself or gotten in a car with the wrong guy.

The cops were looking for him because of the fire but that he was gone from home was not widely known. Nothing in the papers or on TV, no missing kid postings. Just some word of mouth, mostly in the Elkins' neighborhood. Robbie's parents had kept quiet. They had to be frantic, though. I'd just finished drafting a motion for a client on a drug possession case, when from nowhere, like a thunder boom, the words came to me, Wildcat Canyon.

Wildcat Canyon runs from Berkeley to the El Sobrante line. It's the nearest thing to a forest we have. Edged by blue collar neighborhoods on the bayside and rolling hills to the east, the creek meandering through the canyon feeds a thick canopy of willow, dogwood and bay laurel.

The canyon was the scary place talked about in whispers at sleep-overs after lights out—so dark and so quiet, poison oak-ridden; the name itself a warning—a dangerous, biting animal could end you. Coyote, bobcat or wildcat, take your pick. Wildcat Canyon made nightmares. No kid went in alone.

If you wanted to hide from everyone, though, including the cops, it might be an answer Robbie'd come to. There was good cover in the foliage, the water in the creek was clean and there were berry bushes for food. But even in June, temperatures would drop after the sun went down. With the bay winds rushing the leaves and the night noises of animals—growls and scampering footfalls—the canyon would seem filled with menace. If Robbie was in there, I prayed he was warm and had shelter.

As soon as I could get away from the office, I went home and changed into woods clothes. I was going into the canyon to look for Robbie. I drove to the canyon entrance nearest my place. The city had made a little park there, with picnic tables and an adobe BBQ pit. It was an hour before sundown when I started along the main trail. I picked up a thick, gnarled branch on the ground for a weapon.

I was alert to any movement or sound as I descended the trail into the canyon. Sunlight wavered as the overhead canopy grew thick. I tried to avoid the poison oak. As I got near the creek, buzzing insects got louder.

The absence of city sounds and the dimming daylight spooked me. After a half mile, the main trail diverged into tributary paths. I took each to its end, usually a quarter mile or so, then retraced my steps and took another. I kept looking for signs of a human.

Dusk fell. I froze every time I heard rustling in the brush. Civilization felt far away. I was about to turn back, discouraged my hunch hadn't turned out, when, at the end of a narrowing path that choked off into a thicket, I heard what could've been a cough. I peered ahead and about twenty paces to the left.

In the gloaming I saw what looked like a cardboard lean-to against a tree trunk. The piece of cardboard was good-sized, with a vertical seam down the middle. It looked like a thrown-away appliance box. Folded at the seam against the tree, with some sturdy branches arrowed into the dirt and pressed upright along the cardboard, it was a barricade. I squinted at it, trying to make sure the evening shadows were not deceiving me. I walked closer. "Robbie," I whispered once, then a little louder.

I approached very slowly, to not cause flight or alarm. A haggard, pale boy's face leaned from the hem of the make-shift den. Robbie. I toned it soft. "Hi, son. I've been looking for you."

I kneeled a yard or two from him so he could more easily make me out. He recognized me. "I'm not feeling very good. I've been scared," he trembled out.

"I bet," I said. "Let's get out of here. I saw Mags a couple of days ago. She's been scared and your mom and dad are, too. Can you walk?"

"Yeah, but go slow; I haven't eaten much," he said.

I put my arm around Robbie's back and under his elbow to give him support as we walked to the car. The trail was hard to see as night came. With my free hand I banged my stick against trees to make enough noise to keep animals away. We panic stopped at a coyote's howl not far off. Robbie was weak, but we had to keep moving.

My mind went in circles as I planned for what came next. Robbie needed food and water, his mom and dad needed to know he was safe, and the police were looking for him. We got to the car and I gave him a bottled water. It was gone in a long swallow.

"Let's get you something to eat and talk a minute before we do anything," I suggested. "You need to get home and then deal with the cops. I can be your lawyer if you want, no charge, so what you say is between us." I don't usually work for free, but I go pro bono when kids are in a jam.

"Ok," he exhaled quietly and paused, "Ok." I started the car for the drive toward town and he leaned back against the head rest. My heart broke that a boy had so much on his mind he'd run away to escape it. Robbie seemed relieved to be in the car, safe, on our way to eat and to go home, that a thing too big for him was over.

He started to talk. "I had my jacket but it got

so cold at night and I was hungry all the time. I was really afraid about the animals. I heard their noises. I was worried they'd get through the cardboard at me. I heard their claws on it. I knew I was in trouble, but I didn't know what to do."

"We'll get things straightened out," I replied, trying to comfort him. If he knew he was in trouble, then I knew he'd set the fire and an arrest was coming. I'd have work to do.

I turned into a drive-through and got burgers, fries and cokes. Robbie gasped at the cooked smell of the burgers when the girl handed me the bags of food and the drinks. I passed Robbie a burger and I hadn't even parked before it disappeared.

I parked in a slot facing the Avenue, away from lights in the lot. We ate in silence for a bit, just looking out the windshield into the night, at the storefronts and the cars going by. As we started on a second round of burgers, I said, as I always do with clients, "Why don't you just start at the beginning and tell me what happened. I came looking for you because I thought you might be in a fix, but I didn't think you would do something without a reason I could work with."

Robbie took a deep breath. This was hard. "There was some stuff in a file at school."

"What stuff?" I asked.

"I talked in a class too much," he replied. "I got sent down to Clark's office. He had a file in front of him. I guessed it was my school file. I could see some of it upside down. There was a paper stapled to the inside cover with my birthdate and address and things. At the bottom it said adopted."

He turned his face away to look out the side window. He didn't want me to see the water in his eyes.

"Mr. Clark told me I had to quiet down in class or he'd send me to stand in the bike yard during recess, but all I could think of was that word. What did it have to do with me? I got a rushing in my ears. It felt like a rip opened up inside me that won't go away. I've just been sick."

"I got home and I was just too scared to say anything to mom and dad or Mags," Robbie continued. "I couldn't even say the word. It felt like everything would change if I said it." Robbie struggled to put deep, frightened feelings into expression.

"If I got rid of the file the word would go away," he went on. "I knew getting rid of the file couldn't erase whatever happened in real life, but I wanted the word to go away."

With a rush of words, Robbie confessed the fire. "If I broke in the school, I couldn't take all the files. If I just took mine and maybe a few others, they'd figure out sooner or later it was me. I couldn't think of anything else but a fire."

He explained how he did it. "I told mom and dad I was going to the playground, but I went to the garage and got the gas can for the lawnmower. I took it with some matches to the school and pried open a window to the office. I got in, splashed gas around the floor where the files are and back to the window and climbed out. I threw a match on the gas and it surprised me, it whooshed up right away. I started running, blind scared. I got rid of the gas can in a dumpster. The only place I could think of to hide was in the canyon. I knew I couldn't stay there forever, but it was all I could think of to do." His voice had started to quaver. Robbie stopped speaking.

I tried to process all Robbie'd said. I couldn't imagine his confusion and anguish. It was a kid's brain thing to do, to burn the school to get rid of a file. But burning the school was way smaller for Robbie than the adoption bomb. Its crater inside him left him suffering. Three nights in Wildcat Canyon, a reckoning coming with the police and, more importantly, he was about to learn close-to-the-bone truths from his parents that would change who he'd always thought he was.

I tried to ratchet down the tension. "What you've done is serious but not grave," I said. "You've damaged property but not people. You may have to go to juvie for a bit, but I'll work on that. Right now, you have to see your folks and Mags. They're in pain, like you. You have to pull the sliver out to get better."

"Alright," he sighed. "Let's go home."

Before heading that way, I took another minute with him. I'd worked some adoption cases. The new parents always puzzled when to tell their child about being adopted. Kids like security and certainty. Adoption's a mystery to kids. It turns things upside down.

I shifted in the car seat so I could look at Robbie straight. I didn't want to lawyer him, but I did want to help shape his thinking before he went home.

"Robbie," I began, "Have you ever doubted for one second your mom and dad love you more than life itself?"

"No," he said firmly. "I love them, too."

"Ok," I continued, "I hope you listen to this. I've worked on adoptions. It's hard for moms and dads to know the right time to tell it and it's a hard thing to know how to say."

I wanted to be direct with Robbie about what he'd done and what he was facing. "Maybe you weren't ready. You found out and set fire to the school. Not a grown-up way to act."

Robbie was quiet, taking in what I'd said. "I really messed up at the school," he said. "Is everyone mad at me?"

I gave him clarity. "This story will follow you. Some punishment is coming. A lot of kids were excited to see the school on fire, but you can't be proud of it. You have to be sorry for it."

"I still have questions for mom and dad, but I almost don't want to know," he replied. "Does that make sense?"

"Of course," I said. "Every adopted kid feels the same. It's like with Santa. You want to know if he's real, but you don't really want to know if he's not. C'mon, let's go home so you can deal with it. But, Robbie," I asked, "when you first see your mom and dad and Mags, just love them, and keep your heart soft." He looked down, tacitly acknowledging.

As we came near Robbie's house, I could see neighbors in the yard and on the sidewalk. They'd been spontaneously assembling in the evenings since learning Robbie was missing, in concern and sympathy. Robbie's mom and dad were sitting in porch chairs, looking bleak and distracted. A police car was parked across the street.

I let Robbie out a couple of houses down so he could gather himself as he walked. I parked and stood outside my car to see the reunion. First one neighbor saw him, then another. A murmur of voices began that got louder as Robbie came closer. His steps were a little hesitant. It was a precipice moment.

His dad saw him and jolted out of his chair, running to Robbie. He lifted Robbie off the ground, hugging, holding tight. Robbie hugged back. There was clapping and exclaiming. Robbie's mom was seconds behind her husband and when his dad let Robbie down, she went to her knees and wrapped him up. There were no words exchanged, just embraces.

Mags came out of the house at the commotion. She walked over to Robbie and they smiled slowly at each other, a little self-conscious, then giggled. Sibling code, I imagined.

Robbie pointed me out to his mom and dad, who waved and I signaled putting a phone to my ear that I would call them. I walked over to the squad car and told the officer I was Robbie's lawyer. I promised I'd surrender Robbie in the morning at the station. He nodded ok. I got back in my car and drove off, Robbie and his folks and Mags still on the front lawn, reunited, a family, encircled by their neighbors.

I called Robbie's dad in the morning. I told him Robbie had to be booked on suspicion for the fire. He choked up a little thanking me for finding Robbie and for being willing to help on his case. "We're all going with him to the station," he said. "I'll meet you there," I replied. I was glad they were going together.

I asked if Robbie told why he'd run. "He did and it was emotional and we're working through it," Robbie's dad said, probably understating the startled shock of those first few revelatory moments alone as a family after Robbie's return.

"My wife and I hardly ever thought about Robbie's adoption," he explained. "He was a day old when we brought him home. We never knew anything about Robbie's biological parents. As life went on we didn't bring it up. He'd always been ours. We never imagined he would find out himself."

"I'd forgotten the school even knew about it," he continued, "but when we first registered him it came up and I guess that's how it got in the file Robbie saw. We're so sorry how much it hurt him and he was scared to talk. That's that we're working on. His mom and I are holding him close with lots of touch and affection."

All families have stuff and going through hard things together makes strong cement. From what I'd heard, it sounded like a wound was starting to heal. It felt good.

When I got to the police station, Robbie and his family were huddled on the sidewalk, looking a little apprehensive. A couple of news stringers loitered outside the station doors. One walked up to the family, but Robbie's dad waved him away.

I parked and walked over to the family. I said hello and spoke to Robbie. "This won't take long. You're a juvenile. They'll book you on suspicion for the fire, print you, and give you a date to see a judge at juvenile hall. Then, you can go home." I could see the concern in his eyes, but he was being a brave boy. I squeezed his shoulder in reassurance.

"I'm taking him in," Robbie's dad said. They started up the entryway together. At the door, Robbie looked up at his dad. His dad gave him a smile and put his hand tenderly on the back of Robbie's neck. They turned toward the doors and walked through.

John O'Kane

Alchemy

He kisses the redial on his phone once again and orders another draft from the waitress, feeling like he's becoming conspicuous sitting at the end of the bar near this open bay window to the sea, but gets no answer. Yesterday she choked his messages with questions and appeals and he couldn't get back to her fast enough.

"Waiting for someone?" asks the waitress as she delivers another frothy special.

"Somewhere in cyberspace... I'll be leaving soon. Guess I got sorta settled in and lost track of time. "There she is... that's her!" he exclaims, craning through the window to get a better glimpse of her torso skating by on the boardwalk, but snaps back into the waitress's entreating glare. "I guess not."

"She the one you were with a couple weeks ago?"

"Probably... we met here." He stares at the phone like it's a telepathic subject ready to offer its secrets and redials again, propping it up against his copy of the local paper. Maybe her phone's on silent or she forgot it. Gazing out again at the bodies streaming by he imagines what she looked like the last time they met and eco-sketches details into the various versions when a woman beelines through the front door. He reaches for her arm as it passes but she glides past his reach down the bar and disappears before he can catch a glimpse of her face. He redials again and waits.

"Who's this?" a female voice asks, but it's one he doesn't recognize. It's higher-pitched and more frenetic than what he remembers. "Who are you? What do you want? Hello!"

He hesitates, listening to the garbled background chatter for cues about where she is as he peruses the bar for the woman who cruised by. Suddenly, there's a spurt of noise somewhere between a gurgle and a giggle and the call is abruptly terminated. He instantly redials and continues to look around the bar, his visual field interrupted by the waitress's inquisitive glance. Repelling her attention, he jerks up from his seat and steps down the bar for a different vantage while redialing, the extended droning pelting his consciousness like a mocking message. He cancels the call and slips back to his roost, chugging the rest of his draft.

"She pretty important to you or something?" asks the waitress as she arrives ready to retrieve the empty glass.

"She... could be. I'm not..."

"... easy come easy go on the beach, especially when the weather makes you wanna let it all hang out." The words throb in his mind like a neon sign as she stoops slightly to get the glass, her downward tilt jelloing a few more inches of bulge.

"The eyes can play tricks on you." He redials from the periphery as the jello retreats and settles, a droning stretch suddenly terminating.

"Did I just see you? Are you at the Bistro?"

There's no response. The sounds in the background are different now, like the waves are trying to clash. Is that her talking or someone else? "You there?"

"Hi... who's... " A soft thud is followed by a brief tinge of static. Did she drop the phone? Then quickly a louder thud like a body falling on the sand. "Don't let her get away... catch her!" The voice seems to be that of a young male who's out of breath. Suddenly applause breaks out, succeeded by a few shrieks and then catcalls of various intonations and lengths.

"Lucy, are you there?" The sounds become fainter like the activity is trailing away from the phone.

She sits in the lotus position on her kitchen table, mesmerized by the pigeons zigzagging across the leaden sky, their movements somehow in rhythm with her breathing patterns. One finally breaks formation and flits to the ledge, diluting her focus. She takes a deep breath. It seems to notice this change and stares at her for several seconds. She opens the window and cups the bird inside to a table next to the window which contains a plate of seed. Its cheeps pitch through undulating octaves of appreciation and it swivels and bobs toward her while she starts to meditate again. After a few minutes her cell flashes. She tries to keep the intrusion at bay but finally snaps to attention and returns the call. The bird closely observes the conversation.

"Hi, is this... who is this?" she asks, like she's suddenly distracted and can't recall what she was going to say.

"You mean you forgot me already!" the caller spouts. "Has your caller ID gone on the fritz?"

"No, I know... I know. I was going to call you soon. I... I've been trying to relax. The weather's depressing. I have to have sun... more light."

"You'll feel better once you're outside and moving around... that's the best therapy for cabin fever."

"I think I have a... little fever but... I don't think I can go out right now and... be around people."

"I'm not people I'm... remember what we did last night... you said you... your face was... radiant."

"I know... that was yesterday? What did I do? Who are... "

"... you sure you're okay?"

"Yeah, I am... no, no, these walls are closing in but... I've got my companion, my friend... I wanna fly with my friend and be free!"

"Did you stop taking what they gave you?" Her friend begins to flap its wings and utter slightly different cheeps and she perks up, their timbre and structure approximating a message that she thinks she understands. It... wants to fly with me, she muses.

"Lucy, Lucy... are you there?" He hears strange noises but no answer. Is there interference on the line? She swoons, stricken by the bird's alliterating sounds. "Lucy... Lucy... you okay?"

"Who's this?"

"Who do you think it... "

"... sorry, I got distracted. If I could just... if there was just more... light!"

"Let's meet like we planned. I'm across from Big Daddy's."

"Will you be my daddy... take care of me"

"We can... take care of each other."

"Can you give me... 'member what we talked about? That was you?"

"I... I think so. What exactly do you... "

"... you know what I want. Can you give me... "

"... shouldn't we take things a little slower?"

"No, no, I want..."

"... where should we meet?"

"I don't know... if I..."

"... Sidewalk Café bar at five for happy hour."

"Okay, yeah... I want to be with you. I love being with you!" She looks at the bird as it starts to cheep wildly and clasps it in a loving embrace.

Parsing the zones of steamy torpor in front of the Bistro on the way inside, he finds a space near the end of the bar being vacated by a couple and bellies up, retrieving his cell from his pocket and glomming onto it like it's a cocked weapon. He looks around the room for familiar faces but the twilight fumes cast shadows on them, making recognition difficult. And the view of the boardwalk and beyond to the stretch of sand is obstructed by bobbing heads. While making his final perusal he touches the trigger and looks for conspicuous movement since the momentary buzz of merriment would muffle phone noises.

"Thought you'd be off somewhere experiencing romantic bliss," quips the waitress as she glides by teetering a tray of drafts to a threesome nearby.

"No bliss... more of a near miss," he bellows through the din, waiting for her to creep back in his direction. "We were supposed to meet and... well, she didn't show. And after a very promising chat too!"

"I think I saw her yesterday. Does she skate?"

"I've never seen her... but who doesn't along the beach!"

"She was racing up and down the boardwalk and going pretty fast, weaving through crowds of people. She seemed bursting with energy, wearing a constant, euphoric smile but not much else! Her top was looped around her neck like a kerchief. Pieces of her hair were sticking straight out like her body was plugged into an electric socket. She was getting a big crowd around her until the cops..."

"... I doubt if that was her... she's..."

"... you should probably think about changing your dating service!"

She creeps along Andalusia toward Abbot Kinney feeling like the low overhanging branches from the trees are choking her and juts into an alley. Taking a respite on a bench behind a garage, she looks back to see if she's being followed. She's already a half-hour late for her appointment since for the past fifteen hours or so she has had a hard time getting out of bed. Now that she's finally outside in the bright of day the world seems like it's closing in on her. Her therapist will give her something to pick her up if she can only get there. A woman with streaks of pink and purple hair appears around the side of the garage across the way into her frozen gaze and pulls back, bug-eyed, reversing her path. Why is she looking at me like that? A baby raccoon hobbles from the brush near her and scampers up the alley. Maybe my therapist will come and get me! She shakily scrolls down the list of contacts and pins her choice.

"Can you... I can't move, can you come and... get me?"

"Who's this? Is it you... Lucy?"

"Yes, yes, it's... me. Can you..."

"... it's me. Who you trying to reach? What's going on? I've been calling and calling and..."

"... aren't you... can you help me? I have to talk to... who are..."

"... it's me!"

"How did you... I need to get to..."

"... where are you?"

"... I don't know. I have to get to..."

"Where? Hello. Lucy, you there? Hello!"

"I have to... can you come and help me... take me to..."

"... where are you?"

"I... by this garage and..."

"... what are the cross streets?"

"Near... I can't remember. I don't see any signs."

"Are you near Abbot Kinney?"

"I think so."

"Stay where you are. I'll come and... try to find you."

"I have to hurry... I'm late."

"I'm on my way. Keep your phone open. We were supposed to meet the other day at the Sidewalk Café but you didn't show up."

"I... wanted to but I couldn't go out."

"Were you skating on the boardwalk?"

"No... yeah, I like to... it relaxes me. When do you... mean?"

"Recently... yesterday."

"I... don't remember when... they said I should see someone and..."

"... I'm on my way."

So much has happened since their first breakfast at Mao's restaurant. The tables outside were starting to fill with beachgoers, tourists, and workers from the nearby businesses as the remaining patches of gauzy cloud lifted. Specimens from the city's shadow society spilled onto the sidewalk from the alley. A trio of skateboarders trolled by and leaped off the curb in formation, jutting across the street through the horns and screeching brakes.

They peered at each other through a mist of prurience, foregoing direct eye contact for fear of dulling the senses stoked from their newly discovered attraction, or perhaps forcing a premature intimacy that might consume them with mind games and block their mutual explorations that intensified the previous night. They might not know what to say or say the wrong thing, plunging their relationship into oblivion.

"What'll you guys have?" asks the waitress, pulling their gazes out of the mist toward her.

"Oh... I'll just have the commune pancakes and a Tsingtao," he instantly responds.

"I guess I'll have the same, but no beer, just water," she says, waiting for the waitress to slip back inside. "I just took my... medication. It's not really, though. My therapist called it some kind of salt that will... I don't know... make me less active I guess... level me out so I won't..."

"... you do seem different than yesterday," he returns, now managing to look her directly in the eye.

She hesitates and looks at him like she's surprised at who he is, her irises small, flat-brown saucers ringed with a pinkish-white.

"I feel kind of drained, like everything's been flushed out of me. Last night I guess a lot was, and..."

"... you're dressed a lot different and you seem like you're preoccupied. Is something bothering you?"

"No, I... well, about last night I..." The waitress places their orders on the table, interrupting her conclusion, and stares at her like she's anticipating an enlightening comment. Then she breaks away and the waitress twirls to the door. "Why was she staring at me like that?"

"She's probably struck by your... presence."

"The stuff we did last night... I don't know if I can do that... again."

"What... what do you mean?"

"I mean... you know, when you..." She peers away at the cars passing by and then up into the sky. "I can't see... you don't look the same. Everything seems covered with a film and it won't stay still."

"It must be the stuff your therapist gave you. Are you sure it's gonna do you some good? The best things to put in your body are natural... things that grow from the land or synthetics refined from them."

"It helps I think most of the... sometimes I have to give it more time but... it keeps me from getting too down."

"You don't seem like the type that..."

"... once in a while I forget to take it and I... well, I get kinda..."

"... yesterday you seemed more natural and spontaneous."

"But those things we did... I'm afraid of going too..."

"... you weren't on it yesterday?"

"I... got my schedule confused and..."

"... you should purge your body, get off that stuff. It's blocking the real you. How long have you been seeing that therapist?"

"Not too long... probably about two months."

"That's not very long. Who is it?"

"He's really... cool... very sensitive to my needs. A friend recommended him. He reads my palms and has these cards that... he explains."

"Wow... he might be putting poison in your body and messing with your mind. I have a friend who experiments with mind-expanding herbs, natural substances that bring out the true self. They make the body healthier. He has a proven..."

"... I'd like to expand my mind but I don't know for sure what that means. About last night... I can't... go on without... remember what we talked about?"

"I'm not... sure. What do you mean?"

"I need a family and..."

"You mean you want to..."

"... yes... I want to..."

"... but as you said, we don't know each other..."

"... not now but I... need a commitment."

"Well, you need to stop taking that salt... purify your body and your mind will follow. After that I'll get you something that will help you see differently... better."

He thumbs the redial on his cell again as he weaves through the boardwalk amblers, staring at the screen like his visual intensity might conjure an answer to the call. As it goes to message he tries to block out the din in hopes of finally hearing one and gestures futilely at the void. A cold draft swaddles him as he approaches the Bistro and he follows the floating patches of low cloud inside. Suddenly all traces of sun are gone and he takes a seat at the end of the bar. The crowd is sparse, as if the sun-worshippers can't face a day without Hyperion's full streaming.

"Well, long time no see, stranger!" blurts the waitress as she hustles through the door from the patio with orders. "Any luck in locating your skater?"

"Not for a while... and been wearing out my phone again." He raises his cell and grins, thumbing the redial in exclamation.

"I haven't seen her since that time. Like I said, you need to get a new dating service."

He places the phone close enough to his ear to hear her answer and at an angle to his face so he can see the screen and waits, but this time there's not even a message. The cyber-blips stretch on until he finally cancels the call, staring flush into the screen like it might still be possible for her voice to register in defiance of technology.

The waitress, tray-less, slips onto the stool next to him. "I've got a short break coming. What's the latest in this drama?"

"I saw her about a week ago... she called me. Actually, she was calling her therapist and buzzed me by accident. Thanks to her shaky hand and the luck of the alphabet. She was lost in an alley and wanted her therapist to come and get her, bring her to his place so he could give her... something to get her energy back. I'd already gotten her to dump some palm reader who was giving her these salt tablets to... supposedly... even her out. I got her to stop taking those but she's been very uneven ever since, doing some pretty strange things. Anyway, I went to the alley and she was nearly unconscious on a bench. She wanted me to take her to her therapist and I agreed but when we got there I had a bad feeling since he gave her all sorts of pills with strange names. I pulled her out of there and told her to hang on a little longer and to definitely not take anything else until she purified her system. I set her up with this friend who experiments with mind-expanding natural substances."

"You mean like... mushrooms?"

"Yeah, but more like the derivatives from peyote... mescaline. He's kept up with all the research and has been trying to refine and perfect them for years. He works out of his pad above a garage behind Clubhouse. It's full of vials and canisters and smoking kettles and... lots of curious odors. He said she came by his place not long after that and he gave her his latest concoction. His name's Krassly. Know him?"

"Yeah, I think I do. Has long wiry hair and a pockmarked face?"

"That's him."

"I met him through my friend Rhoda who lives on Clubhouse. But I've never taken any of his substances."

"They smooth you out and relax you... get you to see better and relate to people better and more equally. Not the spacey journey into your mind's recesses that most people think. No side effects and... they're not addictive."

"You sold me. But I can't imagine what it might do to your... beach goddess."

"It's the chemical answer to the idea that the whole is greater than the sum of the parts. All of our mental and physical defects stew in a pot and disappear in the cuisine of human improvement. We had some amazing moments when we first met. I can't imagine what..."

"... he can do all of that on a stove above a garage?"

"It does seem kind of... medieval, I suppose, but he's as accomplished as a Nobel scientist. The system's not into his brand of awareness... only profit."

"Hopefully it's not like grandma in the kitchen... little of this, little of that and perfecto... no need for a written recipe. But sometimes she misses a spice or two and the meatloaf flops. What if the subject is allergic or... doesn't get purified?"

The building on Abbot Kinney sits between an upscale boutique and a valet restaurant, and there are no signs or other markings on its facade that broadcast what goes on inside. It needs paint and the windows are boarded up. The dozers could be lying in wait to remove this eyesore. But if from a distance it seems like a dead zone, merely a bridge between consumer spaces, up close it's another matter. On any given day and often into the wee hours you can feel the vibrations as you approach it. And as you stroll by, the sounds radiate from inside: shrieks, wails, yelps, howls, impassioned pleas, testimonials, expressions of unbearable pain transiting through degrees of pleasure toward ecstasy. Some passersby sense that these are from a revival meeting, that the space is a new storefront worshipping venue for those disaffected by the denominations, others that they're witnessing an outbreak of New Age orgy. It's a bit of both, perhaps, and likely all the more reason why its days are numbered. But its designated identity is a place of healing, a clinic. The clusters of health-seekers don't pray with borrowed scripts or to an extraneous spirit, but to a force that bonds souls that need to get their feelings out and revive the intensity of life, one that compensates for too much quiet reflection and restraint. In sharing their edgy emotions in a confined space they can mate or get suspended in loops of hate and spite, forcing a reset.

He slogs through the soft sand in the final stretch of his workout, ducking an errant Frisbee, and plops on a mound above the water. Several surfers deadhead through the roiling water toward the shore and he can virtually feel the tactile sensations from surviving a sated face-off with nature. He decides to get his board.

The clap of a wave delays his response to his cell. The call is from Lucy. He eagerly listens to the message because it has been several days since their last connection. It's barely comprehensible due to the loud background noise but she seems excited, like maybe he's caught her in an upbeat mood. He hastily fingers a reply but checks himself and cancels the call, dropping his head back onto a mound of sand to rekindle his reverie while fighting off the urge to redial. He wonders now what he can possibly say to her. The dashed hopes from the repeated attempts to connect with her have taken their toll, and now that she's finally accessible he can't quite muster the energy. Maybe she's back to... normal or... something even better, he reflects, recalling their early moments together. Maybe she's in trouble and needs help. He hits the redial.

"Is it you, Lucy?"

"Yes... who's this?"

"It's me... you just left me a message."

"I can't... hear you. Who's this?"

"What's all that noise? Who's screaming? Where are you?"

"Hold on and I'll..."

"Lucy... you still there? Lucy!" The noises continue, increase in intensity and then abate. But he can't make out her voice.

"Aiyeeeeeeee... eeeeeee... .ahhhh." The sounds keep repeating, stretching to extreme lengths and then suddenly cease, beginning again in short bursts from what seem like different voices. It stops again and a male voice can be heard.

"See how good that feels," says Dr. Primoff, the Picassoesque director of the clinic. "Look at yourself in the mirror... look. You're more alive now. Your faces, legs, chests, buttocks... I can see the energy seeping from your pores... you've expunged all the poison from..."

"Lucy, where are you... what are you doing?"

"... hug each other now... that's it... that's it. Now..."

"Lucy, you okay?"

"... eeeeeahhhhheeee... no, no... stay away from me, please!"

"Lucy, Lucy!"

"Everybody relax. Back away from her... let her breathe... give her some space so she can..."

"Lucy, is that you?"

"Yes, it's me. Who's this? Oh, oh... are you still there. I wanna talk to you. I'm at the clinic and..." The bursts of screaming cease. A short stretch of silence is succeeded by a muffled then robust round of applause and then supple spurts of tender oohs and aahs.

"What clinic?"

"Dr. Primoff's. I've been here for several sessions and feel... amazing! I can see so much... feel so many new emotions. My body is so full of energy. Your friend Krassly introduced... I saw him last night. He's helping me. Can we meet later?"

He sits in a corner of the Bistro patio still fagged from a late-morning surf but the fatigue seems to be lifting and he's beginning to feel stronger than ever. Pushing his body has done wonders for his muscle tone and stamina, and he's even begun to eat healthier and cut down on substances. The usual low clouds have evaporated especially early and the high sun slanting down from the east seems to burnish and brighten the faces of the strolling tourists, skaters, and nature worshippers. It's like they're being singled out, exposed through a filter that removes all particles of bacteria and smog from the atmosphere, purifying his direct line of vision to them.

"Well, look who slunk in!" spouts the waitress. "I figured you had eloped to some romantic getaway by now. The usual?"

"Orange juice for me and... no, I haven't..."

"... if you're drinking orange juice I guess you're not trying to drown your sorrows so... things must be going well with the..."

"... not... really. I haven't talked to her for a few weeks. Tryin' to get my body back in shape so I haven't sauced it up for a while. Working on a better outlook."

"So it's off?"

"Not sure it was ever on but... it was magic for a short while. She took my advice about contacting Krassly and he sent her to Dr. Primoff's clinic and she..."

"... I know some people who've been there. They came through it with new personalities... though not sure they were better ones."

"Well, she called me from one of her sessions there and it seemed pretty wild. I was looking forward to seeing how her personality might've changed but... we set up a time to meet after that and she..."

"... didn't show!"

"How'd you... you seem to know."

"I've been an off-the-cuff beach therapist for a long time. But you'll see her again. A few weeks aren't much time. If she took Krassly's goodies she's probably... fermenting somewhere. I got some from him last week through a friend. Notice anything different?"

"Somebody call the police... she's indecent!" screams a sixtyish woman as she springs up from her chair at a table on the west side of the boardwalk that's piled with Bibles. "What's this world coming to?" She continues to rant a variation on her themes and a crowd begins to form around her, but they pay virtually no attention to the female she's referring to. The crowd grows larger as three security officers trot down Dudley and confront her. She seems overly excited and begins to stutter, unable to utter clear syllables. As she continues to try she loses control of her body as if she's having a seizure. The furrows in her face become lubricated with tears and she starts to drool while frantically pointing at the female. Seemingly ripe for a straightjacket, the officers coax her to a chair while calling the paramedics. The crowd continues to grow.

"What's with that woman?" he asks while rising from his seat and rubbernecking the scene.

"She's a fixture on the boardwalk... a born again," says the waitress.

"Must be something happening... look at all the people," he returns, shuffling out the door to join them, she in tow.

They can't see the woman who's cocooned by the crowd so they edge around it on the west side for a possible glimpse, but still no luck.

"Maybe we'll read about it in the paper," he says, shrugging off the adventure as he notices the left edge of a body protruding from a tree ten feet or so toward the water. The person, whose back is flush against the tree, begins to speak to a male a few feet away and he realizes it's a woman. Though he didn't hear the short interchange clearly, it must not have been very welcoming since the male moves on. As another male approaches her, he shuffles around the tree for a glimpse of the mystery woman and sees that she's reading a book, *Ulysses*, the only inanimate object attached to her person. Her taut skin is perfectly tanned, the reflection of the sun giving it a golden hue. She has yellowish-blonde curls that cascade onto her shoulders and pastel blue eyes that catch the light as she ever-so-slightly shifts position when turning a page. Her long legs are upright, framing the book, and partially covering her large, firm breasts from his angle. She's totally relaxed and absorbed in the reading, evidenced by her self-satisfied smile. He moves in front of her, seeing her now fully exposed and familiar as the officers appear, stopping ten feet away to ogle. A few more males drift by amid the exploding cacophony of demands from hysterical voices for her to be arrested.

"Lucy... Lucy, what are you doing? Where've you been?"

"Oh, hi! I... that's not... my name. I'm Penelope."

One year later. He drifts to shore on his surfboard, comes to a brief rest and springs up, gazing at the gallery of sunbathers before dashing off fifty push-ups. Invigorated, he rushes up and over the mound of sand to discover a phalanx of shaved heads sitting in the lotus position. They're all wearing gold, loose-fitting unis, and there appears to be no basis for discriminating between male and female. None of its members appear to notice him as he trudges through the sand toward the boardwalk, veering around the left side of the group; they stare straight ahead as if they're in a trance. Then a figure near the rear flinches from formation but quickly jerks back into focus. He stops and gives the person a long look, hoping to re-stir some interest, and steps closer. It seems like a woman but he can't be sure. He steps yet closer and she, or he, turns sharply toward him like when a person tries to catch someone staring at them. But this is a look of supplication, of the desire to say something meaningful. Convinced now it's a woman, he notices the pastel blue eyes in her lingering look. She's heavier and without hair but there's no doubt that it's her. The loose-fitting clothes that hardly do her justice can't hide her bulging stomach.

"Lucy, or... Penelope... what are you... doing? I haven't seen you for a long time. How have you been?"

She looks slowly away from him and nods toward the bulge with a radiant smile.

"My name's Hester now and... I've got a new family!"

Evan Howell

Red Wings

At Mr. Wells' request, Lionel rose from his seat and walked to the front of the classroom. He uncapped a whiteboard marker and began to work on his assigned problems—multiplying fractions. He tried to write carefully, but his numbers came out an uneven scrawl. He was good at math but struggled in situations like this. He'd get so focused on the thought of his classmates' eyes boring into his back that he couldn't think straight.

He had two equations to work. He managed to get through the first and was in the middle of the second when a coughing fit started in the back of the classroom. It was Josh, of course. He hacked loudly, like he had gravel stuck in his throat, and between coughs he inserted his favorite word.

"Dickweed."

That had been Lionel's label since arriving at this school. He assumed it was some type of North Carolina slang. His face burned red. He hurried through the second equation, knowing he'd done it wrong. He turned and started back to his seat, eyes on the floor.

"Not so fast," Mr. Wells said from his desk at

the back of the room. "Take another look."

Lionel returned to the board. He looked at the problem but couldn't focus. All he could hear was snickering from Josh and the other baseball players.

He stared at the whiteboard for a long moment, frozen.

"What's seven times four?" Mr. Wells said, his tone impatient, as though he couldn't believe it was his lot in life to teach mouth-breathing pre-teens who couldn't even do multiplication.

Lionel's mind was blank. His fight-or-flight defenses had hijacked any higher order thinking abilities.

"Seven times four is twenty-eight," Mr. Wells said. Then when Lionel wasn't quick enough to move, he snapped, "Write twenty-eight. We don't have all day."

Lionel wrote it down. As he walked back to his seat, he heard Josh once more.

"Dickweed."

This time it was plain as day, not even hidden between coughs. How did Mr. Wells not hear it? As Lionel took his seat, he glanced at his teacher. The assistant baseball coach sat reclined in his chair, beefy arms crossed and resting on his protruding belly. He had a half-smirk on his face, as if trying to suppress a laugh.

So, he had heard it.

The bell rang five minutes later, and Lionel filed out with everyone else. As he fiddled with his combination lock, Valerie Robinson took her place beside him, accompanied by the citrus smell of her shampoo. She was a blonde-haired, freckled cheerleader in Lionel's math class whose locker sat next to his. He was infatuated with her, but they'd only spoken once all year, a couple months earlier when she asked him what the pages were for that night's homework assignment.

As Lionel dropped off his books, a voice behind him said, "Don't you need to be in some kind of special class?" It was Aiden, one of the hangers-on in Josh's circle. Mocking Lionel was how he asserted his in-group status. Lionel pretended not to hear and, thankfully, the kid kept walking.

Pre-algebra had been the last class of the day, so he loaded his backpack. He went slowly, in case Valerie had another question for him, but apparently she'd written down her assignments that day.

Lionel walked out to the bus lot. He found a seat near the front and leaned his head against the window as the bus pulled out of the parking lot, the glass cool on his forehead, the rhythmic bumping of the ride soothing. He watched the strange North Carolina landscape roll by. So much different than Florida. Down there he could breathe, surrounded by 360 degrees of open geography. Here the horizons were shorter, hills everywhere. He felt claustrophobic.

This was his second year in North Carolina. He'd arrived at the beginning of 6th grade, when his mother relocated to be near a boyfriend. That relationship ended soon after, but she liked the Carolinas enough to stick around. She'd held down a steady job the entire time, working as a receptionist at an urgent care clinic. Lionel was used to her job-hopping, so the stability was a welcome change, to open the fridge and know there would be food. But other than that, he hated it.

For someone who'd spent his whole life in a tropical climate, the winters were miserable. He shivered at the bus stop in his thin fall jacket, wrapped himself in a blanket inside their drafty house. The neighborhood wasn't great, either. No kids there, or at least no kids that played outside. Yards were unkempt; neglected dogs paced angrily on short chains. The police were a regular presence. Lionel's father lived back in Florida and had yet to follow through on his promise to visit.

When the bus pulled onto his street, Lionel saw a familiar red Corolla in his driveway. He groaned. Randy stood at the counter when Lionel came in. Lionel's mother had recently given him a key, which he took as an invitation to drop in whenever he pleased.

"Hey pal," he said. "Got off work early. Thought I'd cook dinner for you and your mom."

He wore a polo shirt tucked into pleated khakis. His pants ended an inch above his shoes, revealing white socks that even Lionel knew didn't match the rest of his outfit. He worked in the billing department at a nearby hospital and his work badge was still clipped to his shirt.

"What are we having?"

Randy pointed to grocery bags on the counter. "Picked up some ground beef. Taco night."

Lionel offered a polite half-smile. He dropped his bag on the floor and went to the fridge for a soda. He loved being a latch-key kid. His two hours of solitude after school were his favorite time of the day. Today Randy ruined that.

Randy was his mother's new boyfriend. They'd been together a few months and so far he hadn't distinguished himself in Lionel's eyes. Lionel was a tough customer, having seen a string of boyfriends over the years, all of whom related to him in different ways. Some attempted to be paternal, while others acted like he didn't exist. There was the ex-football player who tried in vain to teach Lionel to throw a spiral. Then there was the car salesman who smacked his mother around and, just to keep things interesting, Lionel on occasion. As for Randy, he talked a lot.

"Look what I brought," Randy said, putting a familiar box on the table. "Want to play Settlers of Catan?"

Lionel most certainly did not. After the day he'd just had, he wanted to sit on the couch with a Coke and a bowl of microwave popcorn while watching Westerns on cable, but clearly that wasn't in the cards. He joined Randy at the table, too polite to complain, but hoping that his lack of enthusiasm would signal how he really felt. Randy, however, seemed immune to social cues such as sour expressions and he happily went about setting up the board. Even though they'd played before, he explained the rules in detail.

And the lessons didn't stop when the game began. When Lionel tried to trade brick cards for sheep cards, Randy asked him gravely, "Are you sure you want to do that?" This was followed by a lecture on the importance of resource diversity, with Randy opining that sheep were one of the least valuable items in the game. Furthermore, how did he plan to build roads to connect his settlements if he had no bricks? Lionel had never met someone so passionate about board games.

An hour in, his mother bailed him out by arriving home. Randy left the table with assurances they would play more another day. Lionel didn't doubt it.

The evening was one long slog of talking. The adults yammered while they sat around the table, then yammered some more while they gathered on the couch and watched a TV singing competition.

Lionel finally got the peace he wanted at 9:00. Randy had left and his mother was back in her bedroom. He got all set up on the couch with his Coke and popcorn but was asleep within minutes.

A few days later, Mr. Wells handed back their unit tests on fractions. Lionel got a 98. He felt quite good about this, considering that most of the class bombed it. There were no congratulations from Mr. Wells, just the grade scribbled in red ink across the top of the page.

Lionel's attention drifted during class. Mr. Wells was introducing their next unit on decimals, which Lionel found as easy as fractions. As long as he didn't have to demonstrate at the board, he could do these in his sleep. A poplar stood outside the classroom window and he watched a pair of squirrels chase each other around the trunk. He drew the scene in his notebook, the tree branches and bushy-tailed rodents spilling over his half-finished notes.

He'd spoken with his father that weekend. They hadn't talked in nearly a month, so Lionel called. When asked about coming to North Carolina, his father sounded excited about the prospect. He said that his schedule would free up in the fall, maybe he could come up and they'd do a Panthers game. He didn't have much time to talk, but told Lionel to call him the next day and they could make plans.

"Don't get your hopes up," his mother had said when he hung up.

She was right. When Lionel called back the next day, his father didn't answer. He waited a few hours, then tried again in the afternoon. Still no luck. His mom, seeing how this affected him, tried to cheer him up by ordering pizza for dinner.

"Randy could take you to a game," she offered. Lionel shrugged in response.

Sitting in class, his mind drifted from his father to the leftover pizza. A few slices sat in the fridge, and he planned to scarf them down as soon as he got home. In front of the room, Mr. Wells belabored decimals, going slow for the kids who didn't get it. Lionel pulled his phone out and surreptitiously played a game.

When the bell rang, he shouldered his backpack and made his way to the bus lot. He stopped at the bathroom on the way, making sure to grab a stall. He found it difficult to pee in urinals; they gave him stage fright. Once in the privacy of the stall, he allowed himself to smile. Not only had he gotten a 98 on his test, a fridge full of pizza awaited him at home. Not a bad Friday.

As usual, the bathroom was raucous with middle-school antics. When he'd come in, two knuckleheads were throwing balls of wet paper towels at the mirrors. Lionel tuned out the nonsense and tried to do his business. However, while he peed it seemed that the noise migrated to right behind his stall. He cocked his head and tried to figure out what was going on when two things happened at once—he heard a loud bang and felt a sharp blow to his back. Someone had kicked the door in, which hit him and knocked him over. He fell down mid-stream, urine spraying his pants and shirt. A group of boys standing at the open stall door collapsed into hysterics.

Josh stepped forward from the crowd of faces and gave him a swift kick in the stomach. They then retreated, leaving Lionel exposed and gasping for air. The entire crowd in the bathroom vanished. Lying with his cheek on the tile floor, Lionel watched the feet scurry out. No one wanted to get blamed if a teacher happened to come in.

For a while, he lay there. As his diaphragm recovered from the kick, he was able to breathe normally. He eventually sat up, zipped his pants, and examined his clothes. He was a mess. He dragged himself from the floor and walked to the sink. He pulled a handful of paper towels from the dispenser and tried to clean himself. When this proved futile, he got another wad of towels, soaked them with water, and mopped them all over his shirt and pants. If he could dilute the pee, it might look like he'd gotten splashed from the sink. Or spilled a cup of water. Anything was less embarrassing than pissing himself.

When he felt he'd managed the situation as best he could, he warily exited the bathroom, ready to dart back in if he saw anyone. The hall was empty. He held his backpack in front of his crotch as he made his way to the bus lot. He knew he was late and picked up the pace, but when he stepped outside, the last of the buses was pulling out. He stopped walking. A chilly March breeze whipped through his hair.

"Dammit."

His mom was at work and wouldn't be able to give him a ride. With nothing else to do, he started the five-mile walk home.

He didn't tell his mother what happened. Even walking, he still made it home before she did and had time to run his soiled clothes through the washing machine. He wanted to rinse away the memory of that afternoon but knew it wasn't possible. The story would undoubtedly make the rounds. When he came back on Monday, all of 7th grade would know about Lionel pissing himself while lying on the bathroom floor.

God, he missed Florida.

And then Randy came over for dinner again. His appearances were becoming more frequent. He always brought something to cook. Tonight it was ground beef patties. Since they didn't have a grill, he browned them in a skillet. Smoke filled the kitchen, along with a charred aroma that didn't whet Lionel's appetite. When he ate his, it was still red in the middle. He suppressed his gag reflex and forced it down with large gulps of water. When finished, he asked if he could be excused.

"Hang on one second, pal," Randy said. "Got you a present."

Randy got up from the table and retrieved a box next to the door, wrapped in brown paper. He set it on the kitchen table. Excited in spite of himself, Lionel tore off the paper. Underneath was a shoebox featuring a picture of work boots. Lionel assumed that whatever Randy had gotten him, he'd stored in this old box. However, lifting the lid proved this assumption wrong.

Randy had actually gotten him a pair of work boots.

"Boots," Lionel said, with no inflection.

"Not just any. They're Red Wings. High-quality work boots. I worked construction a few years after high school and wore a pair of these the whole time."

Randy rapped his knuckle on the toe.

"Listen to that. Steel-toed. You could drop an anvil on these suckers." He gave a quick wink to Lionel's mother. "Not that I'd recommend it."

When Lionel was slow to respond, Randy took one of the boots out and held it up. It was made of dull brown leather held together by heavy-duty stitching. Thick laces were fastened through brass eyelets. They were clunky and ugly. Josh would have a field day if he ever saw Lionel walking around school in these.

"Every man needs a pair of work boots," Randy said. "Never know when they might come in handy."

When Lionel didn't say anything in response, his mother snapped from across the table, "Could you please act a little more appreciative?"

Randy waved her off. "It's alright, Janice. He's worn out from a long week of school."

Normally, Lionel would have acted more excited. He knew he wasn't being polite, but he didn't have the strength to fake it. The day's events had drained him. He took the boot Randy was holding and put it back in the box. He mumbled a thank you and walked back to his room, where he shoved the shoebox under his bed. He lay down and stared at his popcorn ceiling, looking at the brown water spot over where he slept. It mushroomed out like a cloud, with several layers of color, different hues where the ceiling had dried, then got wet again. The landlord kept saying he was going to fix it.

He could hear Randy and his mother down the hall, laughing together. He rolled on his side and pulled a pillow over his ear. Why couldn't his mom ever pick someone that he liked? Like his dad, for instance. He sometimes felt angry at her that their marriage hadn't worked out.

Lionel's dad gave first-rate presents. One Christmas it was an X-Box. Another time he gave a bow and arrow. Beyond the presents, he was just cool. He'd been a basketball standout in high school. He drove a shiny truck with loud pipes. Women liked him. That was a big reason Lionel wanted to spend more time with him, to learn how to be around the opposite sex. His father was at ease with them. Every time Lionel saw him he was with a different woman, always good-looking. Meanwhile, Lionel hadn't the slightest clue how to talk to a girl, let alone attract one.

His dad didn't drive a beat-up Corolla or give lame-ass presents like work boots. The way Lionel saw it, the only problem with the guy was that he lived all the way down in Florida and that his schedule always seemed to be full.

Two days later, on a muggy Sunday night, Janice asked Lionel to run down the street for a gallon of milk. Over the weekend the chill of spring had dissipated and, for the first time in months, he was able to walk outside without a jacket. His second North Carolina winter was coming to an end, and none too soon. He took his usual shortcut through the park to the grocery store, where he used a crumpled ten-dollar bill to pay for a gallon of two-percent.

On the walk back he cut through the park again, across the soccer field and up an embankment. His path was not well lit and while crossing a drainage ditch he stepped into a sinkhole. His right foot squelched into it, disappearing up to his ankle. When he pulled the foot out, it was covered in mud. He clomped the rest of the way back with one shoe heavier than the other, shaking off debris the whole way.

At home he tried to clean the shoe, but to no avail. It was white and no matter how much he scrubbed, the stain would not disappear. These were his only school shoes. He asked his mom if they could run to Wal-Mart for another pair.

"It's 9:00 at night," she said.

"What am I supposed to wear to school

tomorrow?"

"Randy just gave you a perfectly nice pair of boots."

He sighed. He hadn't even thought about the boots since shoving them under his bed. He retreated to his room, knowing he wasn't going to win this one. He wasn't sure which was more embarrassing— wearing muddy shoes or wearing Randy's ridiculous clodhoppers. It was a toss-up.

He ended up wearing the boots. He picked his longest, baggiest pair of jeans, which covered most of them. Now they just looked like ugly brown shoes.

"Don't think they're such a bad gift now, huh?" his mom said when he walked into the kitchen.

He waited until she wasn't looking to roll his eyes. However, in spite of his worries, he made it to lunch without any comments on his footwear. He seemed invisible today, which was about as good as he could hope for. He sat by himself in the cafeteria, sipping chocolate milk and sketching pictures of Iron Man in his spiral notebook.

Even better, there had been no comments about the bathroom incident. Josh and his lackeys were in Lionel's morning classes, but they hadn't said a word. It occurred to Lionel that it was in Josh's best interest to keep that incident quiet. Physically assaulting another student could get him suspended, maybe even kicked off the baseball team.

When the lunch bell rang, he dropped off his tray and filed out with everyone else. He had band after lunch and needed to retrieve his trumpet. He walked down the hall with his notebook open, putting a final bit of shading on Tony Stark's helmet. He was almost at his locker when a familiar voice rang out behind him.

"Hey dickweed."

His stomach churned. He should have known things were too peaceful to last. He kept walking but Aiden—probably at Josh's bidding—stepped in front and blocked his path. Lionel tried to sidestep him, but Aiden wouldn't allow it. He had an advantage of several inches and at least thirty pounds. Lionel stopped resisting and assumed the position, arms dangling at his side, expression blank. He'd tried different responses to these guys and had found that being a 7th grade Gandhi was the most effective. Nothing they said would make him respond. He wouldn't dignify their existence with his attention.

Josh planted himself next to Aiden. Both wore khaki shorts, polo shirts, and sunglasses perched atop spiked hair.

"Get all cleaned up over the weekend?" Josh asked.

Lionel looked past him. There was a clock in the hallway, safely ensconced behind a cage. He stared at it intently. He watched the second hand jerk along, waiting for Josh to be finished.

"Lionel had an accident the other day," Josh went on. "He wet himself in the bathroom."

His voice was raised, like he was giving a speech. Students passing by slowed down. A crowd began to form.

"Well, it was a little more involved than that. First, he fell down with his tiny dick flapping out. *Then* he wet himself. I'm so disappointed I didn't film it."

"You know," Aiden said, "There's still a way they can see it."

"There certainly is." Josh addressed the crowd

with a showman's flourish. "Would you folks like to see a re-enactment?"

They had clearly rehearsed these lines, like a sick Abbott and Costello routine. A few kids in the crowd responded with cheers.

"OK, you've convinced us." Josh gestured to Aiden. "You be Lionel."

On cue, Aiden produced a small french fry that he'd brought from the cafeteria and held it in front of his crotch.

"Did I get the size right?"

Lionel ignored him, still watching the second hand. Shame burned through his chest, but his face was a mask. Aiden turned around and pretended to urinate while Josh pantomimed kicking in the stall door. Aiden collapsed to the floor and yelled in a shrill voice, "I'm pissing myself! I'm pissing myself!"

The crowd of students—at least twenty strong— erupted in laughter. Lionel's discipline wavered and he allowed himself a glance at their faces. They were distorted with ugly amusement, one kid so overcome with hilarity that he leaned against the lockers and pounded them with his fist.

Valerie was there too, standing with a group of fellow cheerleaders. She didn't laugh along with the others, though. Her face was twisted into a look of pity, which Lionel found even worse. Her expression cut him to the quick and, with a decisive movement, he stepped forward and kicked Josh in the shin with the steel-toe of his boots. The blow felt solid, a smooth transfer of kinetic energy from one object to another, like connecting with a baseball on the sweet spot of the bat. Josh dropped to the floor.

Lionel braced himself for a blow from Aiden, but—to his amazement—his other tormentor backed away, as if he didn't want to be next. Josh lay on his side, gripping his leg. His eyes were wide with shock, staring at Lionel's feet.

"Those boots," he said between clenched teeth. "You broke my leg with those goddamn boots."

Lionel saw an opening, a chance to deliver a blow while Josh was laying down. His Gandhi posture had never been about non-violence; it was just his only option. But now another lay before him and he was about to step into it—to deliver a sweet, retaliatory kick to the stomach—when a hand gripped his shoulder.

"What's going on here?"

Lionel turned to see the face of Mr. Lowder, one of the school's assistant principals. He looked at Josh lying on the floor in pain, looked at Lionel standing over him.

"Come with me."

Josh's on-the-spot medical diagnosis was not accurate. Lionel had not broken his leg, though he did leave him with a sizeable bruise, which resulted in Josh having to sit out that week's baseball game. Lionel received a 10-day suspension. He felt sure the severity of his punishment was related to Josh's absence from the baseball field. Coach Wells had no doubt made an angry trip to the Mr. Lowder's office and demanded justice for his student-athlete. At home that night, Lionel's mother was furious and made it clear that his time off would not be relaxing.

"You'll think twice before getting into another fight," she said, handing him a piece of paper.

It was a list of chores. Washing windows, organizing the shed, scrubbing baseboards, pulling weeds, cleaning bathrooms. He didn't complain, nor did he offer much in the way of defense other than, "He was picking on me."

As expected, this did not fly.

"Son, there are always going to be people like that. What if I go to work and start kicking colleagues I don't get along with?"

Lionel nodded along, pretending she'd made a valid point. In reality though, he knew the kick was well worth it. He'd replayed it in his mind all day and there was nothing he'd have done differently. A lengthy suspension and a couple weeks of indentured servitude were a small price to pay.

When he went to bed that night, he finally took off the boots. He'd worn them all day, even around the house. Upon waking the next morning, he put them back on before leaving his room. He slipped his feet inside and pulled the laces tight. He looked at them from several angles, then ran his fingers over the toes, a layer of coarse leather concealing a steel cap.

He walked down the hall and into the kitchen, his feet making a satisfying clomp on the wood floor. While he poured a bowl of cereal, his mother picked up last night's lecture. He didn't talk back; he just absorbed it, counting down until she left for work.

Once she was gone, he decided to tackle the shed. It was a lengthy task. In their short time in this house, he and his mother had managed to fill it with an impressive amount of junk. He found the work peaceful, though. It was a mild spring day and he walked back and forth, back and forth, pulling items from the shed and dropping them into piles in the yard.

Mostly he liked walking in his new boots. The very thing he'd hated about them only a day earlier—their weight—was now their most appealing feature. It was almost like he'd grown a new pair of feet. Their bulk gave him a pleasant feeling of inertia. When he started walking, they pulled him along. He left larger footprints than he used to. When a rusty paint can got in his way, he didn't feel a thing when he kicked it aside. He felt substantial.

By lunchtime he'd pulled everything out into the yard and decided to take a well-deserved break. He drank two sodas, ate two bags of microwave popcorn, and watched *Fistful of Dollars* from beginning to end, reveling in the joys of an empty house. He'd seen the movie several times, but this time paid more attention to Clint Eastwood's feet as he sauntered around that dusty town, dishing out justice. Clint had a nice pair of boots, too.

He spent the afternoon pulling weeds and working on make-up assignments from his teachers. His mother got home at 5:30, accompanied by Randy. He held a bulging grocery bag and Lionel wondered with apprehension what he'd be cooking tonight.

"Pad Thai," Randy said, as he unloaded items onto the counter.

These words made no sense to Lionel, but he watched as Randy prepared the meal and soon determined it to be some type of noodle dish. It filled the kitchen with a foreign aroma that confused his senses. He couldn't decide if the smell was appetizing or not. When they sat down for dinner, Randy scooped a large helping onto Lionel's plate, then sprinkled crumbled leaves on top.

"Cilantro," he said. Another word that didn't compute.

Lionel took a tentative bite and was pleasantly surprised. This was certainly better than undercooked burgers. As they ate, Janice filled Randy in on recent events.

"Ten days! I didn't know suspensions went that long. I think the next step is expulsion." She twirled noodles on her fork. "Maybe you can have a word with him. I don't think he's listening to me."

Randy looked to Lionel, giving him a chance to state his case.

"They were picking on me."

"He just keeps repeating that," Janice said. "As if that justifies it."

"Your mother's right," Randy said. "You can't go around kicking people you don't agree with. That's not going to get you very far."

Lionel nodded without taking his eyes off his plate. A silence followed. Lionel knew he was supposed to respond with a statement of remorse, but he wouldn't. Janice sighed, disappointed that this conversation wouldn't be any more productive than previous ones. She got up from the table to refill her water and when her back was turned, Randy grinned at Lionel and gave him a quick wink. When Janice returned to her seat, she launched into another speech, this time about how colleges looked at more than just grades. Behavior mattered, too. Randy didn't say much else on the topic, only interjecting when prompted.

"Suspensions will stay on your permanent record. Isn't that right, Randy?"

"Yes, I've heard that's true."

Otherwise, he left the lecturing to Janice. Lionel's muted response took the wind from her sails, though, and after a few minutes she wound down.

"We'll talk about this more tomorrow," she said, putting her napkin on her plate. "And you've got all the dishes tonight, Mister."

As Lionel scrubbed plates at the sink, he

wondered about Randy's wink. What was behind that? It was a knowing gesture, as if Randy grasped the justification for Lionel's actions without needing to be told. Somehow, he just knew. Maybe Randy could relate to being picked on. With his small frame and geeky demeanor, it was easy to imagine him having a rough go of it in middle school, too.

Lionel glanced into the living room, where his mother sat with Randy on the couch. His arm was draped over her shoulder and she leaned into him while he casually flipped channels. Perhaps Lionel's mood was influenced by the surprising tastiness of dinner, but he had to admit that Randy was growing on him. The man had annoying mannerisms and wore godawful white socks with khakis, but he also treated Janice well. Lionel had never seen a man cook for his mother before. And in the six months they'd been together, she was more at ease. Her perpetual anger—at their lack of money, at Lionel's father—had dissipated. She laughed more and yelled less.

When the dishes were done, Lionel wandered into the living room. He stood for a while and watched TV. The news was on, adult drama that meant nothing to him, just idle chatter. He waited for a commercial break to interrupt.

"Want to play Settlers?"

Randy turned towards him, his face shining with a broad grin.

"I knew it would start to grow on you. It's an acquired taste, but once you grasp the strategy, it's hard to stop." He kissed Janice on the cheek and got up from the couch. "Sorry, honey. Duty calls."

Randy was wrong about one thing. Lionel still hated Settlers of Catan. It seemed to him like a bizarre form of homework. However, he liked Randy's attention. It nourished him, the same way his peaceful day at home had, and the feeling of his foot on Josh's leg.

They played for over an hour. When Randy went home at 9:00, the game was unfinished and they left it out on the table. Randy got assurances that no one would disturb it.

"Lionel's got an eight-segment long road," he said, with an excitement that wasn't shared by Janice. However, she agreed that the kitchen table could remain monopolized by the game for as long as they needed.

Once Randy was gone, Lionel went to bed, worn out from working all day. As he tried to fall asleep, his mind flashed forward to his return to school. What would it be like going back? Josh would be angry, that was for sure. But it didn't worry Lionel. The whole baseball team might kick his ass and Valerie probably still wouldn't talk to him, but this bothered him less than it would have only a few days earlier.

His room was stuffy and he got up and opened the window. He stripped to his boxers and lay under a thin sheet, listening to the night sounds of crickets chattering and cars whooshing by and distant dogs barking. He flipped over his pillow and lay his cheek on the soft coolness of the other side.

He looked forward to tomorrow. Another day at home, making his own schedule. The boots stood next to his dresser. Grass stained, creases forming where they bent, already starting to look broken in.

Jhon Sánchez

The DeDramafi

I grabbed Alberto's wrist and explained to him the difference between the *DeDramafi* and a watch: "The orange bar indicates that your body is acting abnormally." I told him that the *DeDramafi* helps us deal with the drama queens.

He didn't believe me, even though his arms looked as if they'd been stung by a jellyfish. "I must have an allergy," he said as he showed me his arm, laying it on the office's kitchen counter. Obviously not; the *DeDramafi* was acting in Intervention Mode. Funny how confused he was. With his eyes open so wide, he resembled the cartoon that he had designed for NightAware, the anti-nightmare medication. The poster with the cartoon was right behind him, and it was almost like a self-portrait. It wasn't that he came from Mars or something. He had come from South-America. But he was a painter, so I guess he didn't care about *DeDramafi* countries. Still, I'd never met someone who didn't have at least some kind of idea about what one of these things does.

During the past couple of days, I'd been hoping that Alberto's bar would turn from orange to the normal blue, so he wouldn't be in Intervention Mode. I voted against it because I don't like to put people in Intervention Mode, but I hadn't checked my *DeDramafi* since the previous night. And this morning, I found out that most of the people in The Circle voted in favor. I looked at my *DeDramafi*, and it had the notification: *Alberto Santa Cruz is in the orange.* It's not fun at all to be in Intervention Mode. Plus, there's a lag time and sometimes you don't even know you're in it when the symptoms start. When I was on, I couldn't sleep. I thought I had insomnia, but it was a doctor who told me as he checked my *DeDramafi*, "Cristina, you're in Intervention Mode, so you know the rules... Until you stop thinking about all this drama..." He paused, as if waiting for me to understand on my own. "Doc, I lost my job."

"Stop it. I don't have time for this." He showed me his *DeDramafi* and proposed to the Circle to keep me awake and sleepy for intervals of 10 minutes. It was like depravation of sleep. He did it right there in front of me. Well, luckily, through a friend, one of the few willing to be seen with me, I got this job as plot controller for this advertising agency and more importantly, I kept my mouth shut without any complaints, and soon I was sleeping again. No more Intervention Mode for me. But Alberto was in Intervention Mode for sure.

So, here we were at the office that Wednesday after Thanksgiving, Alberto with his hives, making these cute gestures, his lower lip hanging, pink and moist, that along with his thin upper lip made the shape of an inverted heart.

***

I kept pressing, trying to show him how the *DeDramafi* worked, but he didn't pay any attention and went on talking about the strange things that happened to him that day. Of course, I liked to listen to him because his stories were so dramatic. Well, I shouldn't admit this, but sometimes it feels like that's the main reason we have the *DeDramafi*: to prevent people like me from being entertained. Drama is contagious, or, at least, so they say. But I liked it and took a secret guilty pleasure as he expressed his worries by rubbing the palm of his hands against his well-trimmed beard. I imagined his jaw tickling the nape of my neck. Oh boy. When I imagined these things, I had to breathe deeply and make my mind blank to continue with whatever I was doing. Many people madly in love got the Intervention Mode, but it's love holding the reins. Nothing wild. This is safe from drama.

Well, he told me first about the birds. He thought the super had finally done something about them.

"I don't know what they call them 'supers'. They're supers of nothing."

Even though I liked to hear him, I had to interrupt, "Alberto, the more you talk like this, the more drama you create, and The Circle is going to come up with something else to decrease your drama."

"My drama?" He stood up paced back and forth across the kitchen. The receptionist entered then with her empty mug. "She accused me of being theatrical, can you believe that?" he yelled, pointing at me.

The receptionist stayed in the doorway but then stepped back out, fleeing the way she came.

He turned to me, leaned over the table and talked just an inch away from my nose. It was adorable.

"Shame on you," he said, and I could only think

about how he smelled of pine. "Just because I tell you what happens with my life..." He poked my chest with his finger. "You, who live in a dull life where nothing ever seems to happen with you. Don't you have some heart to listen to me, to anyone for just a second?"

He now talked in an exaggerated voice to the ceiling, "In this country, nobody listens to anyone." His eyes watered, and he looked away to the coffee machine before adding, "The worst is the itchiness, and it's only here along the arms. Look." He showed me his arm. "I could die, and you would never care. Nobody cares."

"Alberto, please. That's why we have this little thing called the *DeDramafi,* required by law because we are a free drama country. The *DeDramafi.*" I repeated, pointlessly pronouncing each syllable and emphasizing the word *drama* in between.

In a jaw-dropping moment, he kept shaking his head and went right back to telling me his trouble-causing stories, about his super, and the woman who cut him in line at the train, the awful taste of his yogurt, and the office elevators that don't work to his standards.

I placed my hand over my mouth to keep from laughing.

When his hives hadn't disappeared after a week, he was slightly more curious about what I had been trying to tell him.

"My first *DeDramafi* was my mother's gift when I was twelve. Well, like everybody, of course, at twelve, I don't know why, a coming-of-age thing, I guess. Using it was very easy for me."

I even told him what my mother said that day: "Never take it off. It sent a signal to your brain.

Without it, your brain will be in pause." It wasn't death or anything like that but like a blackout. "I've never done it," I explained to him. "But in school some students did it to be free from The Circle, and they fainted right there. When they came back, they say it was like being in under a shiny light without being able to blink." Everybody was scared.

It was unclear, despite his nodding, whether any of this was making any impression on him, and I tried to imagine how I had learned to manage my *DeDramafi* back then. "Compare your orange bar with the people from your Circle." But Alberto just stared at me. I explained to him that the people in The Circle were all our relatives and co-workers and that we always kept an eye on each member. "It all started with the #FreeDrama movement." Of course, he confessed that he had never read the manuals when it was slapped to his wrist upon entering the country.

"I thought this watch was a kind of visa instead of a stamp on the passport." He rotated his wrist, observing the *DeDramafi's* leathered strap, square screen and alarm buckle with the note: Don't Remove. Brain functions will cease.

Of course, it's like an admission ticket to the USA these days. You can't get in without one. A large part of the #FreeDrama movement had been built around stopping foreign dramas in particular from being brought into the country.

I bowed a little, so he could have a better view of my breasts and slowly sat next to him. Those black eyes, slightly slanted, always burned into my nipples. I brushed up against his biceps just once as I tried to explain to him the Intervention Mode. But I guess I was too brief because he went on telling me about his ex and the same story of how he came to the USA.

It was a full soap opera, similar to the Mexican ones that were abolished twenty years ago because of the way they put people in distress. His *novela* went on and on, and I knew that the Intervention Mode wasn't working.

"How could a person change their mind just like that?" Alberto said with a glimmer in his eyes. At that moment, another employee was pouring the remains of some tea in the sink. When he heard Alberto's prattling, he rolled his eyes and slid his pinky across his *DeDramafi* screen before leaving the room.

Outwardly, I rolled my eyes as an indication that I understood the other employee, but I didn't want Alberto be punished and turned into another mute moron without any story to tell. When the guy left, I carefully checked my *DeDramafi*. I clicked the report icon and all the members of The Circle had normal blue bars. The report looked like a flag with blue stripes across almost all the same numbers, except Alberto's. His was an orange blinking bar. He was in the hypersensitive mark.

The receptionist who had come for coffee, laughed when he saw Alberto's rash but when she heard him speaking, she crumpled the paper cup instead and covered her ears with her hands.

Okay, in the office we all know Alberto's story by heart. Anyhow, Alberto had traveled all the way from Colombia to marry his girlfriend and kept repeating, clasping his chest, "I even denied being Catholic. You know I was afraid that they wouldn't allow me to get in this country."

The immigration officer had said, "Good, because otherwise we'll send you to the immigration judge."

Catholics can get some sort of waiver, so they don't have to carry the *DeDramafi*. And let me tell you those Catholics are real drama queens. Well, Japanese are even worse. They want somebody to say 'sorry' all the time for everything. All religions promote drama, Pentecostals get even crazy, talking in tongues, a translation of hysteria from heaven, it seems to me. That's why they all live in the ghetto, fighting all the time for things like taking someone else's seat, forgetting to attend your mother's funeral, or slamming the door. Nobody hires them, nobody wants to work with them. I don't know how they survive. Anyway, let the *DeDramafi* deal with it without blaming anyone. We're in a *DeDramafi* country where we can say anything without fear that anyone could be offended. Of course some do, but we put them in intervention mode, that's all.

But Alberto was a drama queen. Oh boy, he went on telling me about coming to meet his fiancée, the way he carried his luggage and knocked on the door, his dreams of the wedding while riding the cab from the airport, the places where he wanted to paint her again. Oh, yes, he was a painter in Colombia. He went on and on with that bullshit. Then he found her with another man.

Okay, I thought. That's what we have the DeDramfi for. You didn't need to involve more people in this problem and if you started doing it, The Circle would vote for an Intervention Mode. No dramas. But Alberto went on,

"She kicked me like a dog."

"So, what? That's her right," I said, but he was so immersed in his drama that continued talking.

Alberto spent three days locked in a hotel room,

crying for his girlfriend. This is difficult to believe, but it made sense because he didn't have a Circle; otherwise he would have been in the Intervention Mode at once. Three days of crying. Three. What a waste of time. There used to be a time when people didn't go to work from having a broken heart. They took antidepressants, saw a psychiatrist, and some of them took their own lives. Ridiculous. How much money did that cost? Something that was very simple to solve. We voted in The Circle to put the person in Intervention Mode, and the person would start thinking about something different than his problem.

After the break up, Alberto got a job at the office as an illustrator. He had been here for six months now and, of course, I was curious about Alberto Santacruz, the newest member of my Circle. We were new to him too, his very first Circle. He didn't know anyone to form a Circle with, except his girlfriend, but a Circle of two never works.

The first time I saw him, he entered the kitchen talking very fast. He shook hands with each one of us. It was nine in the morning, so the kitchen was quite crowded with at least six of us, from illustrations, editing and public relations, who clocked in more or less at the same time. He said that it was the most wonderful day of his life.

"Because it's today," he kept saying with his hands up.

It was then when he stepped back and bumped into fat Pearl from Public Relations who was entering the room. He turned around and looked at her as if he were sizing the spare tire around her stomach. He rolled his eyes and said,

"I'm so sorry, but next time be more careful when you're coming in."

"Not a problem, but keep cool. No need to overreact."

"Overreact?" He said loudly and went on accusing her as if she had brushed his butt on purpose.

As Pearl staggered away, somewhat shaken, Alberto and I looked each other in the eye. I drank my coffee and went to my cubicle where I checked my *DeDramafi*. Of course, Alberto Santcruz's bar was beyond five, the orange bar was blinking with his name.

Days later, in the elevator, he was talking to someone, I think the young intern from the commercial department. He was telling her that he had some birds in his apartment window. He had asked the management office to chase the birds away. He took the day off to wait for the super.

He drew his breath and released just before going on, "He never showed up. I called the office and you know what they said? 'Okay.' Not even sorry." His face was red; his eyes were bulging. He looked like an angry frog.

We all burst out in laughter.

After all these stories, all this drama, it was a week before The Circle put him in Intervention Mode. We had a lunch party on Thanksgiving Day. He was saying some very weird stuff like,

"Instead of celebrating Thanksgiving we should have an Apology Day for the mass killings of the Native Americans."

Nobody said anything. There was this long silence after that, and some people were already checking their *DeDramafies* to see that all the bars were normal. Of course, that made everybody uncomfortable, but he didn't understand that this was impolite that it was inappropriate to talk about racism, war, massacres, and things of this nature. People can get argumentative.

I took a bite of my pumpkin pie, and someone asked him how he came to this country. Of course, most people expected to hear about the description of the plane, the delicious crackers the airline gave him, the sanitizing smell of the airport. The normal stuff. Big mistake. He started to tell the story about his 'ex.'

"She promised to wait for me. But the worst was that she didn't say, 'I'm sorry I made you come all the way from Colombia.'"

Pearl, the whale of Public Relations yelled from the corner of the table, "Dear, that wouldn't solve anything."

When I came back to my desk, I checked my *DeDramafi*, and I got the message. Pearl was proposing Alberto Santacruz for Intervention. A real bitch. She wrote the same thing they write in those cases,

"Even if it's just one person suffering in a company, the whole company delays. We are *one* and the energy has to be channelized to improve production." Blah, blah, blah. You know it isn't fun to be in Intervention. You wake up, and you don't know what happened to you. You only get a message in your inbox twenty-four hours after it has started. The idea is that you keep wondering what has happened to you. A call for introspection. But twenty-four hours is long time. So, I didn't want to vote for it, but I saw his orange bar. Mine was at one, his was, like, at twelve. Something horrible. I immediately voted, 'No.' It took them almost a week to collect the four hundred votes required for Intervention.

In the scheme of things, this was a long time. I have seen cases less serious than Alberto's where people had voted faster. A month ago, for example, a clerk refused to eat cake at one of the company celebrations because she didn't want to get fat. Of course, the Whale called immediately to put her in Intervention Mode. They desensitized her tongue. Maybe we overdid it. No taste for a whole week to stop somebody from making others feel overweight. Still, reactions can be especially swift when there's food involved.

But with Alberto everybody was delayed voting. It wasn't that we didn't care. I guess everybody was enjoying the holidays, and that's the advantage of being in DeDramafi countries: no need for trials, investigations, scapegoating, accusations, and no money spent on guilty verdicts since at the end of the day we are all guilty of something, aren't we?

So, as I said before, it was this Wednesday after Thanksgiving that I came to the office during the break, and he was in the kitchen ignoring his cup of coffee and watching the red marks across his arms as if they were maps. This is where the story began.

I had to explain to him about the orange bar, and I showed him my screen that indicated that he was in Intervention Mode. I repeated that he couldn't remove it because he would turn into a 'mummy.' "No brain functions. The only way to safely remove it is if you go out of the country, to Mexico or something."

I told him how people in The Circle voted for him to have a rash on his arms. I know I wasn't supposed to show him my *DeDramafi,* but I was sad for him.

I squeezed his shoulder. "You're so dramatic about... everything." I bit my lower lip. "'Specially about your girlfriend—your ex-girlfriend—so people decided to vote–"

"All of this because I told you what that bitch did to me." He turned around and yelled, "Nobody has fallen in love and that's why they're envious." He laughed. "It cannot be true. You got me."

"It's true." I nodded, looking him in the eye.

"So, a bunch of people decided that I had this itchiness?"

"Not me, but more than four hundred people in The Circle."

He let his arms drop, exhaled soundly and leaned heavily against his chair. "You're kidding."

"Look." I showed him my *DeDramafi*. I clicked on the inbox and read him the message of what Pearl had suggested,

'Hives like an allergy. It always works and is not life threatening."

I scrolled down to the number of votes from The Circle: 562.

"How do you know if it works?" he asked me with an air of smugness. "I still like who I am and don't plan on changing."

"We don't. We just guess. In the past, therapists have given electric shocks to cause positive thoughts. It may not work at all. But it's like training a dog not to poop on the carpet. What do you do? Rub its nose in its own shit. So, we try to teach a lesson and change one of those physical manifestations or give you one extra, like those hives. The rest is to wait and see if you change or not and otherwise keep at it.

"No way!"

He asked me questions about the science and technology of the device, but I didn't have any idea. "It's a signal to your brain. It's like a psychosomatic message or something. The only thing I know is that it works differently in each body. Once they turned me into an insomniac for a couple days until I stopped complaining." I put a coin in the snack machine slot and grabbed a package of butter cookies. "Please friends," I talked to my *DeDramafi* playfully, as if the people from The Circle would listen to me, and I went on, "Never suppress the smell of cookies for me. Never. Pleeeeeease." I looked at him and said, "The Circle can do anything: create a shortness of breath, wheezing, permanent nausea. They can vote for anything really."

"They make you sick?"

"Not sick, sick. Those are just hives. Sometimes it works so well because we found the real reason of the problem. Menstruation out of schedule associated with anger. Other times, not so much. But in those cases your mind would be busy thinking about what happens to your body more than your *ex*." He tried to interrupt me, but I didn't allow him. "It's like what happens when you are hungry. You don't have time to think about other things in life, if your boss yells at you, if your neighbor plants a tree too close to your garden, if a pedestrian crosses the street on a red light. You are hungry."

"That's absurd. Everything has drama. We need drama. We create conflict. Besides when I'm hungry I think more about her."

"Stop it. I know it's so effective that all women in The Circle have their menstruation synchronized. If someone is out of schedule, it sets the drama alerts." I took a bite of my cookie. "These are so good." I swallowed. "Enjoy life. If you continue with the drama... The *DeDramafi* always measures sweat alterations, heart beat increases, and body temperature changes. If they continue to be abnormal The Circle is going to alter a body sensation. Maybe nausea when you smell cookies." That was a really bad joke because I love my cookies, 'specially after lunch. "Just kidding anything but the cookies, for me."

But after all, I was right. The Circle was already voting for another sensation alteration.

"Look." I showed him my DeDramafi again. I wasn't supposed to show him at all, but someone had proposed a new suppression.

"Eliminate the taste of coffee," Pearl as always came up with the most unique punishments.

I love this one. It's different; don't you see? Not the regular itchiness. I voted in favor of the suppression. It makes perfect sense since he was drinking black coffee almost every break.

It seemed fair to mention, "I don't know what is going to happen exactly to you, but you are going to find that coffee tastes like water."

He lifted his strong chin with that cleft and laughed.

Well, I let him go. He didn't have any idea how the *DeDramafi* worked, but I understood 'cause he came from a country without *DeDramafies*. I returned to my cubicle, wondering what it would be like to live in a country without *DeDramafies*. Should we say sorry all the time? Still, if nobody tells them to stop the drama how the hell can they stop it?

I was reviewing the text of a commercial, making sure that it couldn't be considered an apologia for crime, violence, or anything that can perturb people, when I found Alberto's eyes fixed on me with a frown that formed a Chinese-like symbol on his brick-like forehead.

"What have you done?" he yelled, showing his mug with black coffee.

He sat looking vacantly.

"So, where's my right to privacy?"

"Privacy? You were the one who was talking about your girlfriend all day."

"But I had the right to decide–"

I had to explain everything again while he gulped coffee as if trying to get out of a bad dream. I told him about The Circle and how everything was more efficient without dramas, apologies, tantrums, how we got the *DeDramafi* for our twelfth birthday because we're a world free of brats, how it all started with one of those Freud-type guys who said that drama queens feel guilty and want to be punished, how we formed a Circle of friends and coworkers who know how to punish the person in question, causing a physical sensation. "Please never remove it. You can turn into a vegetable without it. Temporarily. But you don't want that."

He was in shock, but I went on, "We don't even have lawsuits." Well, that's not entirely true, but most of us don't need to blame anyone–except Catholics. Muslims too, now that I think it over. That's why we don't have any Muslims here. They have to ask for forgiveness any time they kill an animal. I think other religions practice similar things, but I don't know much about it except that they live in those ghettos.

Alberto kept asking why it had to happen at twelve.

"I dunno," I said, thinking on another butter cookie. The truth was that I never read a book that analyzed the problems of self-esteem, but I was glad to live in a country where our girls don't need to have tarantulas for eyelashes, wear practically nothing and make duckfaces instead of speaking up. I didn't know for sure that that's how the girls were in Colombia or Mexico, Non-*Dedramafi* countries, so I tried to be diplomatic.

"I guess before 12, little children don't take offense very seriously... They change moods very quickly." Children are the real dramatic ones though; that's why parents had to entertain them all the time, acting like clowns.

Alberto left my cubicle with his hands on his head, showing the hair of his knuckles that I always wanted to yank.

I don't remember what the suppression was that worked out for him. Maybe it was the coffee, but, in any case, everything was working well. I was amazed. I checked my *DeDramafi* every day, and no person in The Circle had rated out of normal. No drama. It was quite sad because at the end of the day I liked to think about what Alberto was dealing with. I thought that maybe in Non-*DeDramafi* countries people charge money for their disgraces. Some people like me enjoy listening to drama queens no matter what. Anyway, everything was normally boring.

But one day, I saw him in the kitchen again. We were alone because I had to work late, and I was eating a chocolate chip cookie even though I wanted a butter cookie, but resigned myself to it because I wanted my *Dedramafi* to issue a normal report, free of drama.

I sat next to Alberto and saw how his hands were shaking. He started rocking in his seat, and he was muttering over and over, "I killed somebody."

I checked my *DeDramafi*, and he had an orange bar that looked like it was about to explode. Oh boy! I sat next to him because I wanted to hear another story. I wanted to have the opportunity to massage those shoulder blades that form perfect triangles. But I held his hand on my lap. Then, he told me how he met this old dude in a coffee shop. He tried to include him in his DeDramfi's Circle of friends, but the screen rejected it even though all the information was correct.

"You can't just put anyone in your Circle. The Circle is your coworkers and relatives, people who *know* you," I said.

Rocking in his chair, he went on telling me how they, he and the old man, met in a bar near Union Square. "It was like I was talking to my father." This was quite important because Alberto told me that he grew up without a father. They ended up pretty drunk. Alberto insisted on giving the old man a ride to his house. And, of course, Alberto smashed his car against the wall. It was an instant death.

He stopped rocking. "And nothing happened."

"What do you mean?"

"The police came. My insurance attorney showed up with a bunch of papers I signed right there while the police were taking some pictures. Blood was still seeping out from the passenger seat."

"Wow," I said in solidarity.

"I wasn't arrested or anything. I was completely drunk, and the police yelled 'go home,' while I was telling them that I was sorry."

The point was that in *his* country if this happens, you go to jail, and you ask for forgiveness, you need to cry and put on a whole show. How lucky we don't have anything like that. The insurance comes and pays everything. Well, he came from a Non-*DeDramafi* country. Can you imagine being blamed because you spilled a cup of coffee on someone's arm? Here the insurance pays. That's all.

Another employee came to the kitchen. Someone I'd seen in public relations. He put a coin in the snack machine and selected a bag of potato chips. The machine made this *wuppa-wuppa* sound like a helicopter, and the bag got stuck. He punched the machine and shook it but realized what he had done; he looked at his *DeDramafi* and sighed. It seemed that his anger was so brief that the *DeDramafi* hadn't picked up the signal.

Alberto checked around to see if anyone was watching him. "I don't want someone to tell on me, so that I end up in Intervention."

This made me laugh, and I told him, "It doesn't matter. They know that something is not right because of the report based on your blood pressure, heartbeat, sweat and so on. Hiding would never work at all."

Again, he didn't listen to me and wept. I almost couldn't make any sense of what he was saying. Somehow, I understood after he blew his nose that it was because he was Catholic, and instead of going home and taking the day off, having a nice dinner as any sane person would have done, he decided to go to the funeral home. He entered, and even though he saw the closed casket, he demanded that it be opened. What? To see the smashed face of the old man? Of course, nobody listened to him. He lurked around, waiting for the widow. When they brought her in, he described her as "A tiny old lady. She looked like a doll being propped by men that seemed like giants by comparison."

Alberto wanted to approach her and apologize, but the security personnel removed him. He was fool enough to even sign the guest book as 'the guilty killer.' What the hell, I thought, but didn't say a word.

"I only wanted to hug her and say, 'I'm sorry I killed your husband.'" He pouted his lips—so cute that I wanted to bite them. He kept repeating, "Why did they do that to me? Why?"

I took a deep breath. "They *removed* you because it is essential to not inflame the conflict. That's why we have *DeDramafi* to deal with that stuff." I wanted to say that we don't need divas anymore and people asking for forgiveness.

"If I could hold her hand, look in her eyes, and tell her..."

"Stop it. Her husband is dead and you're not going to bring him back to life–"

"But–"

"I'm talking—you would only bring her more suffering."

"I need to apologize to her. It's the Christian thing. It's the only way to get relief and forgiveness." He wept. "An apology," and he literary howled like a dog.

I shook my head and rested my forehead on my hand, imagining that the orange bar was going to pop up like a Jack-in-the-Box.

I gave him some sparkling water which he spat out in the kitchen sink, saying that I was going to give him something to make him mute without feelings—my mistake, entirely mine. The only good thing was that he washed his head and somehow cooled off.

I explained to him that if he offered an apology—well that was a mess up. "It's like pushing a fallen person into quicksand. It creates more drama." An apology is the most tragic of all dramas because it recreates the tragedy. In Argentina, they have the Remembrance Day for some killings that happened down there. Here we never think about that. The massacres, the slavery, the wars, and even offensive words are part of the past. We always look to the future. What do the Argentinians gain in making all of society feel guilty? Who knows?

Of course, we're considerate of minorities. I heard that Catholics are allowed to offer some kind of mass to get forgiveness or something. That's pretty rare. I think what Catholics do is blame each other. It would have been easier if he had said that he was Catholic to immigration when he entered. He wouldn't need a Circle. But how the hell would he find a job? As far as I know, there are no jobs for outsiders. How the hell does a Catholic survive if they keep looking for the guilty one all the time? Nobody could ever work with them.

Alberto wept and told everyone in the office that he wanted to apologize, even though he had promised me that he wouldn't. His bar turned so orange that it even heated up my *DeDramafi*. So, the problem was discussed as a message in the *DeDramafi*. People in The Circle said all sorts of things about Catholics' need to be forgiven.

* That's weird
* He's sick
* The orange bar has reached 15. We need to act quickly

It went on and on. Some people suggested an arrhythmia, but others were worried that in the past some had actually had a real heart attack. I wrote that I didn't want another rash, and I'd vote for anything that was creative. "Think outside the box."

We hadn't decided on the Intervention for Alberto when he arrived at my apartment. It was a rainy night, and he was soaking wet. I made him come inside and offered him one of my light blouses that he put on after drying his chest. Then, he explained to me what he wanted to do.

"I had to apologize to that lady, the widow."

I crossed my arms. "You don't understand. We're in a *DeDramafi* government. We don't do that. They're going to put you in Intervention Mode. And even if you apologize, the lady is not going to get it. People in her Circle are going to block everything that would stir drama.

"So, what's this *DeDramafi* for?" He yanked at his *DeDramafi*'s buckle to rip it away.

I held his hand and told him that we couldn't do that. "You're going to get forced into a coma. It's really horrible." I struggled to keep him from ripping it off.

Somehow, he calmed down and between sobs managed to say, "I won't be able to return ever to my country with this weight of guilt. I cannot look anyone in their eyes." At this point, there were more sobs. "I hope they put me in jail. I killed someone. That's the normal thing to do."

"We don't have jails any longer," I said, seriously concerned. "We have one single punishment for the most hideous crimes and for those drama queens..." I wanted to say 'drama queens like you,' but instead I explained to him that they could suppress every function and put you into a coma-like state, without any feeling, completely blocked. "The same would happen if you had ripped off your *DeDramafi*."

He looked at me, wide eyed, and pleaded, "I need your help."

I guess he turned me on, so I went on with the plan he proposed: we break into her apartment. You hold her, and I issue an apology."

I thought, if we did this, I could manage my

emotions, calm down quickly and get away without Intervention Mode. If we could act cool, cold blooded, there would be no report. Besides, I also thought that if we did that, maybe Alberto would calm down and prevent himself from getting into Intervention Mode—Well, maybe all of that wasn't true either. Simply put, I wanted to be near him. Love is a roller coaster of emotions, and I couldn't hold it back any longer. I was worried, though, that this was bad for me too, that this would affect my *DeDramafi* report. Well, the problem wasn't that I was in love. The problem with love is not the love itself but the story of love. 'Cristina, don't think he's going to kiss me, don't think he is going to pull me against his body, don't think he is going to marry me. Simply, don't think,' I repeated to myself, sure that this would keep my report straight and low.

I drove him there. Entering the apartment building wasn't difficult at all. It was a Saturday—which was good because most people rest from checking their *DeDramafies*. We got into the building behind visitors who were carrying some gifts with red ribbons. I guess the guard thought that we were going to the same party. We got to the eleventh floor, and knocked on her door, but nobody opened. That was the idea: knock, wait, push the door forward after she opened it. But nobody opened the door. We needed to break in. I was afraid for any alarm that would go off or neighbors who might see us. But that wasn't the big problem. It was how we were going to open the door. Alberto took out a fucking pencil.

"Are you kidding me? It's going to break. Don't you have a credit card or something?

We ended up using a laminated photo of his ex-girlfriend. As soon as I slid it in, he started yelling.

"Break it! Rip it off! Right in the middle of her nose!"

"Hush," I kept repeating, afraid that one of the neighbors was going to come out.

Well, indeed, we broke the card, leaving a web-like pattern across his girlfriend's face. He snatched the photograph from me. "Ugly witch." Then, he started weeping.

A neighbor next door peaked through his door. I really didn't know what he was thinking, maybe he thought that we were from the old lady's Circle or something, because he looked at us from head to toe and without any greeting and with a hoarse voice said, "She's downstairs in the laundry room."

When we went down the hall for the elevator, we heard the speakers announcing that, "two individuals, a man and a woman, trespassed into the building, and they have been wandering around the 11th floor."

We looked at each other and ran, taking the fire escape all the way to the basement where we expected the laundry room to be. We got downstairs, and there she was folding some man's pants over a chair. At first, I thought she was a little child, no taller than a table, until I saw her disheveled white hair.

Alberto knelt on the floor so that his face reached the same height of the old lady. I kept an eye on the entrance as he began explaining, "It's about your husband." His eyes watered, and I talked through my teeth. "Hurry up. Go to the point."

"My husband? Went for a walk to Union Square. Since he retired, he does that every day." She laughed and shook her head. "I bought him these pants, but I didn't realize that he had gained weight." She chuckled. "We're on a special diet right now, but some people warned us that the lack of food might make us emotional–"

"Just leave her alone," I yelled at him, realizing that she was in 'denial mode.' I explained to him that she was processing the seven stages of grief without even realizing what it was she was grieving. "That's very popular with people that suffer a loss." I wasn't part of her Circle, but I guessed they had made her feel cozy, low blood pressure, slow heartbeat, prone to sleepiness. Circles usually like the denial, and they keep the member there for quite a bit. Anger was another thing though.

I overheard some voices coming in. "Hurry up, let's go." It was then that he grabbed her, put her inside a laundry bag and ran towards the exit. I barely had time to say, "What are you doing? Are you crazy?"

Nobody stopped him, even though some people turned around to see him while he was running down the street, and the old woman inside was convulsing and kicking.

When I got in the car, the little thing with her hunched back was hidden below the rear seats, in the space for the passengers to put their feet. She yelled, "My husband is going to call the police."

I was about to tell him to get out my car, but I was floored when he pulled out a gun. It was something small, with a barrel, a metal muzzle like a single dark eye. The truth was that he looked like a cowboy with that gun, even though I think he wasn't holding it properly. The little lady was probably somewhat right when she yelled at him, "My husband is going to teach you how to fire that thing."

First, I drove aimlessly as the old lady yelled, and Alberto fumbled through my glove compartment with one hand, holding the gun with the other. He found a roll of duct tape, and as soon I had to stop for the traffic light, he lifted his leg and squeezed himself into the back seat. I overheard a struggle until the little lady appeared in the rearview mirror with a piece of duct tape covering her mouth.

"Let's go to Mexico," Alberto said.

"Mexico?" I almost swerved the car, but he waved his hands emphatically, telling me that once we got there, we could remove the *DeDramafi*, and she would be able to listen to him.

He was bouncing that gun as if it were a dancing bird, ready to mate. "You told me once that if we go to Mexico, we can remove it." He froze for a moment and spoke as if he were reading the Declaration of Independence, "No more denial or anything. Just free. All of us free."

I wanted to say 'No,' 'Impossible,' 'I have to work next week' but was also aware that I was probably already in trouble: Abetting in a kidnapping. My insurance would be able to pay for all the damage caused, but my premium was going to go up. But I softened slightly when he caressed my arm with the muzzle of his gun, insisting that the plan wouldn't be so bad.

"Well, what the hell. I have full insurance coverage." I shrugged and pressed the gas.

On the highway, two children waved at the old lady from a sedan in the lane next to us. The lady started frantically knocking on the window. Alberto was dozing off, and I had to wake him up to make her move away. The children waved their hands and shook their mother in the front seat, but she ignored them. Thank God. They were underage and without *DeDramafies*, so their parents probably thought that the children were making drama just for the sake of it.

We stayed in motels along the way. I always checked in. Alberto put the old lady inside the laundry bag and followed me upstairs. We would have liked to have brought her in walking, with all due respect, but although she always promised to be quiet, and as soon as Alberto yanked the tape away, she yelled like a mad woman. Of course, anyone who would see her would think that it was pretty strange that a person like that wouldn't be in Intervention Mode.

Sometimes we took naps by the side of the road where the truck drivers stayed. One time in Sapulpa, Oklahoma, the old lady managed to escape. I don't know how because I put on the child safety lock. I guess she was very careful and slid out by the front window that I'd left open.

When we woke up, we ran to look for the lady. I found a truck driver talking to the little thing who was shorter than the man's legs. Really, she was a dwarf.

"Call my husband, please. Call the police. They want to take me away from my husband," she was saying, and I knew she was still in denial... at least somewhat.

"Grandma Olivia," I yelled from afar as the old lady put her hands in prayer.

"Don't listen to them," She begged the driver. "My name is not Olivia."

"Alzheimer's," I muttered to the truck driver who said,

"I guess Alzheimer's is a big problem for you. Don't make a fuss of it." He shook his head and bowed to rub the old lady's back. She was so small that he looked as if he were petting a dog or something. "You know, the *DeDramafi* doesn't pick up the abnormal signals. It's a failure in the electrical transmission of neurons."

"Of course, otherwise The Circle would have already put her into Intervention for making complaints to strangers. Hopefully the next upgrade to the *DeDramafi* will have Alzheimer's features."

After that, we kept calling her Olivia because we knew her last name but not her first name, and she was so stubborn that she wouldn't tell us. She didn't want to eat or talk to us at all. I even had to hold her mouth open so Alberto could pour soup down her throat. We always ended up wet with soup on our clothes, and Alberto, on more than one occasion, held her by the neck, putting his gun on her temple, yelling, "I won't kill you because I need to apologize to you."

But she kept doing it. I was hoping that her Circle would do something to prevent all this drama and make our lives easier—well the kidnapping easier, more humane, if you wish.

I think it was Friday, and we were driving across the desert when I realized that 'Olivia' was particularly quiet that day. She had nodded like always when Alberto asked her if she promised to be quiet. And when he yanked the tape, she didn't even flinch even though I always thought it was painful, mostly for her little mustache that turned pinkish, irritated. I could imagine the stinging sensation as if each hair had been simultaneously tweezed. But she tilted her head, smiled, and she didn't even massage her face.

I pointed to three yellow wires that looked like snakes slithering between a fence and a baby cactus. Olivia and I pleaded to Alberto to return to see the snakes, but Alberto refused. I looked at Olivia with a half-smile. Then it hit me. The *DeDramafi* had been working of course. No drama. The day before we had gone to a diner and Alberto, as always, turned the air conditioner on and put tape on her mouth. She hated the tape. So it was *always* a fight. She would spit on us and move her head. But that day, she didn't do anything. No insults, no spiting. Nothing.

"Good girl," said Alberto. But the real clue that her *DeDramafi* was working was when he took the tape off. She used to yell like a mad lady: "Bruto, animal."

Her eyes were vacant as if they were seeing something I couldn't. It was as if she were high but with this air of sainthood that the Catholics have in their paintings. So, I imagined that her Circle desensitized her skin or something.

Alberto kept saying that once we crossed the border, he was going to rip off the *DeDramafi*, and we were going to be free. The day that the air conditioner was broken I tried to tell him that the people in The Circle were voting to put him in the Intervention Mode. But guess what? He didn't want to talk about it.

Of course, the people in The Circle were wondering where he was. I was imagining that they were also asking where I was too. And even though Olivia was behaving, no doubt I had a lot stress: the kidnapping, the driving, and Alberto's yelling. One of the problems is when we turn into drama queens, but we don't even realize it. And anyhow, I wanted to control myself to keep from entering in Intervention Mode. Breathing exercises always helped calm down the color of bars on the screen. But I needed to see if the Circle had an eye on me.

The problem was that Alberto didn't allow me to check his *DeDramafi*. I didn't want to be in Intervention Mode without knowing. At least, I could be prepared.

So, I snuck into his bed and grabbed his arm as he stretched it out, palm up, against the pillow. I was careful rotating the strap to see the screen when

I heard his chuckle. He grabbed me by my waist and brought me inside the bed. He made love to me that night. Really it wasn't that great—he didn't come at all. He was jabbing and jabbing inside me, and I kept quiet until he sighed, pulled it out and turned gasping.

"Gringa, you don't know how to make love. Get out of my bed." Then he pushed me. I fell and smacked the floor, but, fortunately, Olivia was very sound asleep. I walked away when he called me, "Hey, Christy, you know what happened... those belly stretch marks really turned me off."

I couldn't believe what he was saying and kept thinking that he thought I was ugly. I went to the bathroom and cried. Let me tell you I had years without crying at all. I looked at my stomach and so on from different angles. 'Too many butter cookies.' Then, for a moment, I thought it could be the *DeDramafi*. They may have taken all sexual sensation from his body. I checked the mailbox and searched through recent voting activity. I couldn't see what they had done with Alberto. My signal wasn't working well. Maybe that's why he was like that with me.

Then I remembered the grimace on his face when he was talking and looking at my body. It was as if I were a rotten apple. 'So he really saw me like a defective machine, rusted wreck, a useless tool,' I thought.

The following morning, I checked my *DeDramafi*, and they had a proposal for fixing Alberto: 'Increasing his sweat.' They say that the report showed that he was sweating more than a normal person in The Circle, which I thought was very stupid. We were in the desert. Besides, the air conditioner was broke. Sometimes people in The Circle don't think. What if he's running a marathon or something? I tried to tell him about the vote when I saw the huge beads of sweat rolling down his forehead.

"Shut up," he yelled.

After what he told me last night, I wished I could have voted for his Intervention. I wished he could turn dry as a potato chip. I wouldn't be intimidated so continued talking. He tried to put his right hand on my mouth, and we almost hit a goat. The animal was crossing the road and he had to turn the steering wheel almost 180 degrees and braked.

"Get out of my car," he yelled at me.

I did.

He tossed me a bottle of water and drove away. The sun glared against the sand, and I wished I had grabbed at least a piece of clothing to cover my face. The heat rising from the sand and the gray cement, and came down with the glaring sun. The desert. The Arizona desert was a broiler that would certainly fry me like a breaded chicken. I thought that if I melted down—no pun intended, my Circle would do something.

"Shit," I said as I looked down at my sandals, full of sand. The thing I hated the most: sand on my feet. Well, anything on my feet, cold feet, sweaty feet, dirty feet. Then, I heard the car tires neighing. I turned to look up. Olivia was waving at me, calling me. She held the door open and once I was in, she leaned on my shoulder and smiled.

Once in a while, I checked the *DeDramafi*, but I couldn't get reception. Well, it went on and off. Olivia's had full reception. I guess when you are old enough your Circle is bigger. I didn't think it was the server.

Anyway, the Circle imposed on Alberto was a punishment for all of us. Such sweat! Oh boy, I hadn't seen anybody in my life sweating like that. Olivia and I pleaded to get out of the car, so we could breathe fresh air.

Finally, we crossed the border by foot. It was nothing difficult. The US patrol officers looked at us like we were dumb or something when Alberto wrapped Olivia inside the bag. Did I tell you that she was very calm? She didn't fight or anything. On the contrary, she just got in the laundry bag quite happily and stuck her head out like a puppy. Pure evidence that the *DeDramafi* cured all evils.

We crossed the Rio Grande. You know how I hated to have something on my feet. The wet water, the slippery rocks, and the occasional dirt. The river wasn't deep, and I keep asking Alberto if we could drown, but he ignored me, pouring and pouring sweat. Well, we didn't drown. The water reached the level, at the most, of my knees.

Now, that I'm thinking it over, I don't know why we couldn't have just gone through normal immigration. Olivia was all smiles and for sure she wouldn't have made any fuss. I guess Alberto didn't want to take any risk that she was going to start screaming right in front of the Mexican Police. For Mexicans, the kidnapping was serious. A crime. Something serious like that. Oh boy.

Well, I was almost on the other side of the river when I started to feel worried. My feet didn't bother me. Oh God, I wondered whether the Circle had put me in Intervention Mode. I hurried and went past Alberto to reach the other end.

"Bye darling," said Olivia.

Of course, I couldn't know if I was in Intervention. I might get a message tomorrow. 'Your feet are unsensitized. Drop your attitude.' It was also possible that my feet were numb. I was thirsty, tired, and sore like a beaten dog. I ducked under the shade of the giant transmitter that Mexican use there to keep people happy. It was huge as a tree with the shape of an antenna. I dried my feet, which gave some comfort with hope the transmitter would block Intervention Mode from the Mexican border to here.

Then I looked up, and what do you expect to see if you are on the Mexican border? Of course, Mexican flags like the American flags lined all along the other side. Well, not at all. No flags. What I saw were piñatas. Yes, the ones you see in little children's parties. I managed to count eighty-three, but they were all the way along the border, hanging from the few trees, the electrical posts, and the cactuses.

There were six police officers (or Mexican immigration) looking up at one of the piñatas. One of the police officers shot the piñata. The others ran jumping into each other and laughing.

"What the hell?" I said aloud as Alberto laid Olivia next to me. We were right under a piñata in red, green and white. It was like an eagle or something. Its colors glittered with sun. I drank some water. Olivia was laughing.

Alberto took Olivia's wrist and ripped off her *DeDramafi* and tossed it into the water. He asked me to give him mine. But I hid my wrist behind me.

"Whatever," he said and cut his off with a butter knife.

I'm glad I didn't give him mine. How was I going to return if I didn't have a *DeDramafi* and applying for one, it would be a mess. Anyway, he stood up very solemnly with his hand on his chest. He was no longer sweating. Then he said, Mrs. Kirkiland. I didn't want to cause the accident. I only wanted to bring your husband home. I shouldn't have been drunk or anything."

So she started wailing, and he hugged her. He was crying,

"Please forgive me."

Suddenly, she took out Alberto's gun from his holster. I waved to the Mexican police, but they were playing with their toys and eating candy.

"You son of a bitch. You killed my husband, kidnapped me and now you want me to forgive you."

Alberto dropped to his knees asking for mercy. I closed my eyes when I heard the shot. I felt like some stones had fallen on my body. I opened my eyes, and I saw Alberto and Olivia surrounded by toys and candy. She was laughing and jumping and hugging Alberto. They both were laughing. She still had the gun with the muzzle up.

Then it hit me. Americans are in *DeDramafi* country, but Mexicans are in Tequila jurisdiction. I'd heard about it, that it was some kind of child wave transmission. Even though, I was under the transmitter, the wave hadn't caught me. Maybe 'cause I was still wearing my *DeDramafi*. I was normal, but Olivia and Alberto were like little children. She laughed. He frowned. She slapped him on the face. He tickled her. She cried. He scratched her. So I got out there, and I came right back across the border to America. Who the hell wants to be a twelve-year-old again?

Authors

Hailing from California, **Bob Ritchie** now lives on the lovely island of Puerto Rico, where he discovered, among other things, that wet heat is better than dry. He has a fantastic wife and as many as five kids, depending on the configuration of the day. He does some editing, yeah, some teaching, sure, some translating, claro. Ritchie (as his wife calls him) is also a musician who is fortunate enough to have collaborated with the musician Jon Anderson, a particular favorite of his. As a writer, Bob (as he calls himself) has penned several things that he believes are good.

Gordon J. Stirling is a retired U.S. diplomat, now residing in Eagle Mountain, UT. Following his retirement from the Foreign Service, he was an adjunct instructor in political science at the University of Nevada Las Vegas (2005-2009) and at Utah Valley University (2010-2011). His short stories have been published previously in Carnival, v.3, 2013 and Decades Review, v.14, 2015. "The School's on Fire" appeared previously in Voices de la Luna, V. 11, No. 4, August 15, 2019 and in Fine Lines, V. 28, Issue 3, September 2019.

John O'Kane has published two books of literary journalism and one short story collection, as well as 175 essays, articles, stories and poems. He teaches writing at Chapman University.

Evan Howell is a writer from North Carolina. He's published short fiction in The Rockhurst Review, Relief, Swill, and Blacktop Passages, among others. More information at www.evanchowell.com

A native of Colombia, **Jhon Sánchez** arrived in the United States seeking political asylum. Currently, a New York attorney, he's a JD/MFA graduate. His most recent short stories are Pleasurable Death available on The Meadow, The I-V Therapy Coffee Shop of the 21st Century available on Bewildering Stories and "'My Love, Ana,'—Tommy" available on https://www.fictionontheweb.co.uk/ . His first novelette, The DeDramafi, was published on The Write Launch and reprinted by Storylandia in issue 36. He was awarded the Horned Dorset Colony for 2018 and the Byrdcliffe Artist Residence Program for 2019.

Thank you to the Wapshott Press sponsors, supporters, and Friends of the Wapshott Press.

Muna Deriane
Kit Ramage
Rachel Livingston
Laurel Sutton
Kathleen Warner
Tom Loper
John O'Kane
David Meischen
Ann and John Brantingham
Laurel Sutton
Toni Rodriguez
LindaAnn LoSchiavo
Suzanne Siegel
James and Rebecca White
Alice Frances Wickham
Leslie Bohem
James Wilson
Robert Earle and Mary Azoy
Kathleen Bonagofsky
Phil Temples
Richard Whittaker

The Wapshott Press is a 501(c)(3) not-for-profit enterprise publishing work by emerging and established authors and artists. We publish books that should be published. We are very grateful to the people who believe in our plans and goals, as well as our hopes and dreams. Our new website is at www.WapshottPress.org. Donations gratefully accepted at www.Donate.WapshottPress.org.

www.ingramcontent.com/pod-product-compliance
Lightning Source LLC
Chambersburg PA
CBHW070501130626
46555CB00003B/1105